198
G

GOODBYE, MR DIXON

GOODBYE, MR DIXON

IAIN CRICHTON SMITH

LONDON
VICTOR GOLLANCZ LTD
1974

ISBN 0 575 01875 5

MADE AND PRINTED IN GREAT BRITAIN BY
THE GARDEN CITY PRESS LIMITED
LETCHWORTH, HERTFORDSHIRE
SG6 1JS

GOODBYE, MR DIXON

I

Hᴉꜱ ɴᴏᴠᴇʟ ᴡʜɪᴄʜ was called *The Meeting* had
come to a dead stop at the point where the novelist hero
(middle-aged and alone) was to meet a girl of twenty-five
or thereabouts whose entry into his world was to change his
life.

The problem was that he did not know what would happen
when his novelist hero met the girl. The novelist hero, apart
from being middle-aged and alone and divorced, was also
a bit of a cold fish owing to the fact of his difficulties with his
previous wife who had been demanding and horrible and, in
short, a bit of a bitch. He had one afternoon packed up and
cleared off with his typewriter in order to continue his new
novel which was set in the future and dealt with the White
City and the attack on it by barbarians. He wanted his
novelist hero to be resurrected from the detritus of his life
and be given the last rites of happiness with trumpets, bugles,
church bells, etcetera. In order for this to happen, his novelist
hero (whom he called Drew Dixon) had to meet a young girl
of twenty-five who would put him back on the rails again
after "the mess he had made of his life".

As for himself, Tom Spence, he wasn't really a novelist at
all. That is to say, he hadn't published novels as Dixon had
done : he was an embryo novelist only. He was one of those
people who live hand-to-mouth on practically nothing at all,
but with the determination to have a book, especially a novel,
published. Not even a great novel, just a novel. It is true
that he did live in a flat like Dixon but this flat was paid

7

for not by mandarin novels created by a mind preoccupied solely with greatness but rather by sporadic incursions into the "real world", for example by spells at labouring or any other job that came to hand. It is also true that, like Dixon, he lived in a city.

In fact he wasn't a novelist at all owing to the fact that he had never even brought a novel to a successful conclusion (or any conclusion) though he had in big red notebooks a number of failed and unfinished novels as well as notes for others. He had, however, once published a poem in an obscure little magazine called *Trauma* and in lieu of money had received five copies which he still had in his flat, since he had no friends, because he believed that to be a good writer one had to be alone like Greta Garbo, uncorrupted by the need for "making allowances" which one had to do when one entered "society".

Thus he didn't have much "experience of life" though he often thought that the great novelists didn't seem to need this. After all, what experience of life did Jane Austen have? Or for that matter Kafka, unless one were to take into account working in an office? In any case he had locked himself up in isolation spending most of the day writing, except that now and then he would take a long walk for the exercise.

He didn't even know very much about the world of Dixon who, unlike himself, had been writing novels for a considerable period and living from their sale. Dixon was a successful novelist and had been reviewed in the quality Sunday papers. Dixon wrote interesting metaphysical novels, rather like those of Hesse, which were very arty and symbolic and beautifully composed and shaped. One novel was about a man who, like Gauguin, had gone off to live among primitive people, and the contrasts between the tribal simplicities and urban complexities had been carefully pointed. The new novel was about the struggle between the barbarians and the civilised people in the world of the future. He would have liked to write like Dixon but found it difficult, not to say impossible. Also Dixon had been "in love" with his wife and the parting had been a shattering one. He himself had never been in love. To be in love he considered odd and artificial and sentimental. Better would be to be in lust. There was something altogether too spiritual about being in love. And if one set out to write novels or to be an artist of any kind, one couldn't afford that. The true novelist looked at the world coldly and inhumanly. He would get material even from the death of his dearest one. His eye was like that of a seagull, cold and belonging to the sea. Certainly he himself couldn't afford marriage. And, anyway, everything he had ever read suggested that no writer could be happily married : there were examples of Tolstoy and Fitzgerald, to take only two. And of course he didn't earn enough money to support a wife. And on this he had old-fashioned ideas. In fact most of his beliefs were old-fashioned. He would drink if he had money but otherwise he wouldn't. In fact he was the kind of conservative who wished to write *avant-garde* books but found that there was a stiffness in his imagination such that he found this impossible.

He blamed this stiffness on his upbringing. After all, being Scottish, he could not have the malleable sort of imagination to which the world was plasticine. And his parents too had been old-fashioned and dull, so much so that he had taken the first opportunity to leave them. At school he had been a vague rebel, not passing enough examinations to allow him to get to training college or university. He pretended to look down on "education and all that" but at the same time he was often terrified and alone, and behind his laughter there

9

was the grin of the skull. But then he must maintain his persona, mustn't he? One teacher—who taught English—had told him that he had creative talent and featured him at length in the school magazine with poems written out of a fashionably youthful wretchedness—mostly about death—and this he had taken as a sign, since no other signs were available. After all you were a writer or you weren't: education couldn't make you a writer. How could education make a writer of Rimbaud? (He hadn't read Rimbaud but knew about him.) Thus the phantom notion of writing as a generalised activity had been the banner which sustained him on dreary days when he couldn't understand mathematics or statistics or most of the other subjects he took, and when he stared miserably out of the window at the city landscape.

So, leaving the school, he had found himself with nothing at all he could do except odd jobs at labouring. At Christmas time he worked in the post office as a postman. And the rest of the time he wrote, isolated in his flat. This wasn't really the sort of existence Dixon had led, though he had read on the blurbs of many novels long lists of jobs which had apparently prepared the writers concerned for immortality. He himself couldn't say that he had learned very much from labouring. On the other hand, Dixon never had to do jobs like that: in fact, he wasn't particularly sure what Dixon had done. People like Dixon simply emerged and were immediately recognised as significant. He imagined that Dixon would do most of his writing in a garden in the summer sitting in a deckchair, and in the winter in a large spacious study with lots of windows.

He didn't really know very much about Dixon except that he was an ideal to which he tried to attain, a mandarin who had however been partially destroyed by his wife, and who was now entirely alone working furiously on his "great" novel.

And anyway he himself had now come to a dead stop on his own novel. It had started off well with an interesting idea, the idea that a man who tried to be perfect in art would find himself without knowing it in the middle of a situation which was steadily cracking up and which would eventually confront him with perhaps the breaking of his marriage and style. He couldn't remember how the idea had come to him; it wasn't even part of his experience. In fact he thought that an artist of any value should write objectively, and therefore about experiences not his own. In this, however, Dixon himself was an exception in so far as his present novel was concerned: previously he had written objectively enough about the rival claims of art and life. And even in his novel Dixon was trying to conceal autobiographical facts by means of a fable set in the future.

The problem of art, he was now beginning to realise, was simple enough: how do you learn enough about the "real" world if at the same time in the service of art you remain isolated? How do you get enough experience in such a situation, or at least give the reader the illusion that you have such experience? You couldn't understand the world of the novelist from working in the post office.

Not that his own experience in the post office had been what one would call unalloyed. It wasn't so much the vagaries of the weather that had troubled him, nor even the misaddressing of letters. Rather it had been one particular incident which had made him realise in what a world of airy inadequacy he lived. Every morning he had to go down to the railway station to get a bag of mail which he would then put on a wheelbarrow. Near the time that he wheeled this barrow across, a train was scheduled to pass, and he had been told about this by the stringy woman in charge of the branch office. One morning, however, he had forgotten about the train and his barrow had been struck by it and twisted into a mangled heap. The train had of course continued on its way and he himself, red-faced, had restored the ruined implement to the post-mistress with a feeling of utter despair. At the time he wished that he could have seen the humour of the incident—as of technology for instance smashing up a more primitive instrument—but there hid in him to his cost, as he well knew, a righteous inner being afraid of making a mistake and forever seeing him as a fly to the gods. Thus as he humped his mail from tenement to tenement he kept wondering what they would be saying about him at the office, what brilliant remarks they would have invented as they regarded the defunct barrow. He felt quite sure that Dixon would never have found himself in such a situation. In fact, perhaps that was why he had created Dixon as the ultimate aesthete, perched high above the battle, immune to the ravages of time and accident, obsessed with the beauties of art and the symmetries of the word. Perhaps also that was why he had avenged himself on Dixon by giving him a wife who would smash all that up quite senselessly and remind him that sex was above or below that sort of existence.

Now therefore he sat in his room and stared at his typewriter, having come to a dead stop. The room itself was not a large one. In one corner there was a white cooker beside the sink which was often full of unwashed dishes. Bronze-coloured curtains hung from the window. Beside the cooker and away from the sink was the TV set opposite which he so often sat in uncreative moments watching *Dad's Army* and *Softly Softly*. In a corner beside his chair there was a heap of books and magazines through which he scrabbled vaguely when he had to find notepaper if he ever wanted to write a letter, which he rarely did. On the table were brown paper bags containing loaves and cheese on which he existed most of the time. One of those days he would have to buy a second-hand refrigerator. This world was certainly different from Dixon's. Dixon of course lived in a "beautiful world". He had a large study with all the latest books. He even had a paper knife for opening his mail, which came from all corners of the world. There were statuettes, a piano, sculptures and paintings, especially those of the Old Masters. He himself preferred surrealist paintings, ones which composed themselves out of the dream world and rubbish which cluttered the artists' minds.

He sat at the typewriter and stared at a yellow bottle of Parozone which stood on the floor beside the cooker. The yellow was bright and almost sunny but the liquid inside the bottle was acid and harsh. Perhaps that was what art was like. Some day, he thought, I will write about a bottle of Parozone. I shall write about it as if it were a respectable theme like daffodils. I shall see it as an object in itself, uncorrupted and pure, the acid juice which turns a sunny face on the world. I shall make the bottle sing. And he thought for the hundredth time that he wished he could paint. Painting was much easier than writing. Painting was a gesture in itself, it did not have to survive against heavy odds among the sharkish adjectives and nouns of the common sea. Painting could be utterly pure and bright and naive. Writing couldn't be.

Oh Christ, he thought, I can't do any more just now. He got up and took his coat down from the nail behind the door, for the day was cold. He went out, slamming the door behind him, making sure that he had the key. That bloody woman on the same landing was out, thank Christ. She did insist on knocking at the door and handing in newly baked scones and jars of preserves. He skipped hastily downstairs as if he were about to be pursued and walked briskly along the street, in his tight khaki trousers and long khaki coat whose collar he turned up against the cold wind. And at the back of his mind Dixon continually cruised in his self-sufficient world. It was a good thing he had been banished from it: he would have to find his own way about from now on. Let him see what art was all about. Let him see what he would do if he was confronted by twisted wheelbarrows in a surrealist dream of thin post-mistresses with thin necklaces and thin grey jerseys and whiffs of antiseptic deodorant. Let the bugger work out his own salvation. Let him see if he could find his new found land.

2

Drew Dixon, attenuated, tall, a smoker of endless cigarettes, stared out of the window at the snow which covered Glandon. He didn't like the cold. The cold made him feel more fragile than usual. Behind him in his study were the copies of the works of Henry James whom his wife detested, preferring to read romance stories or books about Mary Queen of Scots and Marie Antoinette, historical novels such as she would find on tables at cocktail parties, and which she would glance at in the passing, while adjusting her hair in front of the mirror.

As he stared out at the snow he was thinking of the ending of one of James Joyce's stories. There was something wrong with these closing sentences, he was sure, there was something wrong with the sound, with the number of syllables. Drew Dixon was wearing a pink cravat; he liked pink and lilac, they were his favourite colours. On the wall behind him was hanging a Victorian painting of an autumn scene. He liked Victorian paintings.

As he looked out he saw his wife coming in from the snow-covered scene. She was wearing a butterscotch-coloured coat with muffs. He often thought how amazingly lovely she was. But he considered her as a work of art. She reminded him of a picture he had once seen on a stamp issued by the post office — some autocratic fine-boned monarch, whose name he had forgotten. Not that he was the kind of person who often thought about the post office. His only remark about it had been, "The post office is an institution that prevents communication. In this it is like language." He thought of himself as a kind of Oscar Wilde. Except that while Wilde was a very good dramatist he was a very good novelist. Everyone admitted that, even the Observer and the foreign papers. His works had been translated into French and German.

He had very long thin fingers but even in cold weather he wouldn't wear gloves. He refused to do this, though he had been in the habit of doing so. On this particular day he knew that his wife was in a bad temper. The reasons for this were complex but one of them was that she was the sort of person who was often in a bad temper. He turned back to his typewriter. He had been writing a story about a barbarian who had just caught a young woman, the daughter of a professor, in a post-nuclear world. The event happened in the brush outside the city of the Civilised Ones, the White City. He worked like Flaubert, a page or less a day, sometimes, on good days, two pages. He was very particular about fining his prose down to a minimum. He knew the exact sounds and flavours of words, like his Master. His only trouble was that he didn't bother about morality: reviewers had commented on this, but in a famous interview given to a schoolgirlish lady from a magazine, he had defended himself: "In the twentieth century morality is not possible." He had made a joke about some work of his which had once appeared in a school magazine and about an English teacher who had said that he would make a name for himself in the future.

On the other hand, Dixon had devoted his life to the word. No one could take that away from him. He had refused to do any work other than writing. He hadn't even been a labourer or a dishwasher, however useful these jobs might appear to the creation of a great novel. He had said, "A great writer doesn't need experience." And his wife was in a bad temper. It is difficult to say why she was in a bad temper any more than usual. Most things put her in a bad temper. Today she started a quarrel for no reason at all almost as soon as she entered the house. She went on about her life, about his life, about the existence he led. Why didn't he ever meet her friends, she demanded. Why did she always have to go out alone? Why did he think himself so superior? Outside, the snow fell, obliterating old prints. He thought she looked very lovely.

It wasn't until a very long time had passed, while he was thinking about the professor's daughter and how frigid she really was and whether the barbarian ought to be given a sophisticated language, that he began really to listen to her. "I am leaving you," she was saying and her face was twisted with hate, or envy. His own face was impassive. All those years of writing had made him cultivate a style, expressionless and animated. She looked exactly like a spitting cat, one of those wild cats that one sees in pictures standing on rocks in the Highlands. He suddenly thought, I don't really like her. And he was surprised by the thought because he hadn't considered her so remotely and dispassionately before. He didn't know where the thought had come from. The snow was still falling remorselessly. He looked out at it and he thought, The snow doesn't write very well. If he could choose some flakes like words ... But the idea faded into the ghastly whiteness. He suddenly heard himself say, "Go to hell."

She had been going on and on about his being a punk writer and an impossible egotist, and he had said, "Go to hell." One thing about him, he didn't have illusions. He knew that he was not yet a great writer but he would perhaps become a great writer, though not with her. He knew that clearly now. He simply didn't like her. She was always interrupting him, she was always needing attention. She was *always going on about things, trivial little things, stupid things. He needed someone else, someone younger, he needed someone who would give him peace. He needed someone who wasn't always competing with him. He thought, what a stupid bitch she really is.*

There was snow on her coat and it was melting in the heat of the electric fire. He needed a fire all the time and the two bars were on. On the floor were little balls of discarded paper, rolled up pages. He looked at his typewriter. It was old and battered. He didn't like new things. He thought, I have never compromised in anything, certainly not in my writing. I should never have married this one.

Now she was saying something about his unsatisfactory sex life. He was thinking quite coldly, how much money have I got in the bank? He knew that he had ten thousand pounds or so, most of it from a film which had been made of one of his books, called Double Vision *though the title of the book was* Doppelganger. *He was wondering, can I leave this apartment? She can have it. I've had enough. Thank God we don't have any children. That moment was the decisive moment of his life. She had stopped talking as if she knew this. She was looking at him with parted lips. He thought, she has become becalmed. He thought, I shall smash her beautiful face. I shall go out into the storm. An orphan of the storm. He smiled grimly. He was quite handsome when he smiled like that. He said, "I'm leaving." And at that moment he knew he must go, this was his last chance. If he didn't go now he would never go. He took the paper out of his typewriter, closed the lid, and putting on a heavy warm coat left the house while all the time she gazed at him in astonishment, in complete silence. He walked across the snow knowing that she was watching him from the window. He was always conscious of other people watching him. He didn't*

18

wave, he didn't look back. He wasn't at all angry, only resolved. He thought of the scene as something he might use in a future book. He caught a bus because he didn't have a car. He didn't know where he was going but he thought that he ought to get some peace somewhere. He deserved it. He deserved some happiness, he thought to himself. I shall send for some of my books, he thought, when she isn't in. And he calmly and quite objectively considered what he had done, feeling quite cold, having come out of the warmth. He felt the cold intensely. As if he had left a cocoon. And yet he looked forward to being alone. Perhaps he could finish the book if he was left alone. Perhaps.

3

A s T o m w a l k e d along the street he was wondering
how Dixon was getting on in his flat. Better to give him a
slum—he himself had once lived in a slum—but a slum
wouldn't suit Dixon at all. When he himself had lived in a
slum (now demolished) there lived above him a Protestant
who, in the intervals of working as a fitter, would go out and
shout insults at any Catholic he could find. Every Friday
and Saturday night he would stagger home with blue stains
under his eyes, beat up his wife (so that he, Tom, couldn't get
to sleep for the noise of crashing chairs) and on the Sunday
morning would emerge airily in his blue suit to go and buy
the papers and read up on the sport. Also in the same tenement there lived a woman originally from Donegal who had
pictures of the Virgin Mary on the walls as well as one of
someone called Emmett. Every summer she would set off
with her asthmatic husband to Ireland where the grass was
very green and people still rode about in carts and they would
return punctually after a fortnight for him to go to work in
the distillery again. On her mantelpiece she had a painted
cardboard structure showing Christ with a crown of thorns
mocked by squat Jews who had the well-fed air of prosperous
Protestants.

No, such an environment would be unsuitable for Dixon.
Better would be a large, airy flat which would have large
windows looking on to a lake of swans so that he would
think of Yeats. In the evening he would stroll gently there,

talking to nice people who owned dogs and lawnmowers and watched a lot of TV.

But the problem still remained. How was Dixon to meet his new love, the one who would save him from himself and allow him the peace and silence necessary for the completion of his "great work"? Tom thought of this as he walked along, at the same time taking in his surroundings which weren't at all pretty. There were walls of tenements with worn ads stripped away, there were closes with flaked paint (usually green), there were men going past with paper bags which presumably contained cans of beer and bottles of whisky. There were little shops where they sold pornography and second-hand detective stories side by side with dairies which sold rotten-looking vegetables in open window boxes. How did these places survive, all these little dingy shops that blossomed briefly and faded, and were eventually transferred to other hopeful newcomers who stayed up all night doing the accounts and making sure that the tomatoes and oranges and Victory V's had come in? A living illustration of Darwin, shopkeepers; puny and dull, fighting each other to death in a warren of underground shops. He passed a window which advertised the most interesting range of sexual positions, and oral sex. A boy was standing at one corner selling newspapers, now and again clapping his hands and whistling through his teeth.

The Art Gallery, naturally. That was where Dixon might meet such a girl. Or a select poetry reading. No, that would be no good. Poetry readings were ridiculous. He couldn't bring himself to attend one of them even for the sake of his novel, all these little concrete poems read by hairy illiterate people with massive egos. Good God, imagine it. Once there had been a Homer and now there existed a being who had written a book called *The Pink Aquarium* or edited a magazine called *Squeeze*. How could the classical sun have descended so low in the sky? No, an Art Gallery was the best place surely. There one might meet such a person, a girl who was lonely and who yet had a respect for Art, who was not odd or ludicrous but who had not yet met the person she might love. Yes, surely the Art Gallery. And he knew for a fact that Dixon was exactly the sort of person who would visit an Art Gallery, never, however, the cinema. Dixon despised the cinema and TV. Tom himself didn't. He loved the cinema, and remembered those poky ones down side streets which he used to visit many years ago, where old men paraded up and down shushing the children at the matinees and spraying disinfectant impartially over the old and the young, the clean and the unclean. Ah, those stiff-lipped prepackaged English lieutenants, eternal boys of the imperial sunlight, saying Bung Ho and things like that, before they raced up to their planes whose propellers were turning on small airfields: adjusting their goggles before ascending into the blue to save their mothers, uncles, aunts from a fate worse than death, protecting the English seaside and the fat women in large red bloomers: saying goodbye to their sweethearts in a corona of blue lamps, and saying Sir to their fathers who were often professors or ex-colonels.

The Art Gallery, that was it. Dixon would go to the Art Gallery because in those canvases everything was fixed, art gave the illusion of permanence and privacy, it did not flash off and on like neon lighting and was not seen in the half-formed names of shops or on the backs of cornflake packets and soup tins. Yes, the Art Gallery would be an idea. He would surely meet her there, strolling about, peering at her catalogue, standing back and studying as if with an invisible lorgnette those pictures framed in permanence, sitting now and again on the sofa provided, tired out by the reds and greens and blues.

He turned on his heel and began walking away from the rotten tenements and steadily as he walked he approached the better part of the city. The brown stone was replaced by grey, the windows bulged outwards and weren't cracked, there were lawns and gardens where there had been nothing but pavements, the streets widened and there were trees. Surely Dixon would like this part of the city. Indubitably. He wouldn't live in the tenements—their noise and heat and glare and intimacy—but here he could live. There would be space for him, space for his imagination to expand in an orderly manner. Here he could find something Georgian in the architecture, a fineness and neatness and solidity and spaciousness that he wouldn't find in the city centre. Here he would be able to breathe. Here there would be tenements with clean well-lighted stairs and rooms with high ceilings. Here there would be children's bedrooms with toys and fairy stories and books ranging from Enid Blyton to Emily Brontë. Here the children would sleep long with their dolls and teddy bears clutched safely in their hands, knowing that their parents would come when they called, that the light was still burning, that the giants on the stairs could not survive parental disapproval.

As a matter of fact Tom himself did sometimes visit the Art Gallery, especially on a Sunday when there was nothing else that one could visit and he didn't have enough money to drink. He didn't, however, care much for Art Galleries though he believed that Dixon did : he believed that Dixon loved Art Galleries with a pure love that knew no fatigue, he believed that Dixon listened with ravishment to the Third Programme, and he believed that it was right of Dixon so to do. After all, surely it was better to love Beethoven than to love Bob Dylan (there really did seem so much difference between them): it proved that you did have a finer mind, that you were in touch with a great culture, that you were a more complex and worthwhile being. He felt that this was absolutely true, he felt that his own fatigue when he listened to classical music was a flaw in himself and not in the music, he did genuinely feel this. He felt that the world was full of better people than himself, who would listen to music like that or study paintings with minds as clear as windows.

But he didn't like Art Galleries. He found them dull and monstrous vaults, his body ached after he had been walking about them for a while, there were too many paintings and they were too different, and he didn't know what to look for in them. He felt that he ought to like them but he didn't. He felt that they might be trying to say something to him, but he didn't know what, and this angered him as one might be angered eventually by a long argument with someone who did not see what one was getting at. He felt that the sculptures—the Davids and the rest—were momentous and monumental and weighty, but they usually left him cold and stony and he disliked himself for that. He felt he ought to like Michelangelo and da Vinci but he didn't, they were too huge, too distant, too weird. They seemed to be speaking to beings who had long since passed away, who had lived noble, dignified lives, aristocratic people, edged and spiked with hauteur.

He stood at the door for a moment looking up at the steps, and was reminded of Eisenstein, a profile of whom he had recently seen on TV. Now *there* was somebody: he could identify with him. He climbed the steps slowly. Sitting at a table in the foyer or hall or whatever, there was a woman with a mouth like the opening in a Barnardo's box, unsmiling and dour. He didn't buy a catalogue but walked in. The woman had looked at his khaki coat disapprovingly as if she thought he were some kind of refugee from Central Europe who ought not to be allowed into her calm halls. She had probably thought he was some kind of tramp. He hated her for this because she was such a stupid woman (he was convinced of this; otherwise why should she be there doing such a silly boring job?). He hated her because clearly she was easily deceived by appearances. She had dismissed him, he felt, without knowing what he was really like.

He climbed some more steps and stood in the main body of the hall. He glanced at a tall thin spindly structure to his left. He didn't have a clue what it was meant to be and toyed with some titles such as "Match in Urinal" or "Fasting Rocket". He stalked around it, wondering whether the bit at the top was supposed to be an attenuated head or a stone berry. Perhaps the whole thing was a stone tree, something heavily symbolic anyway. Dixon wouldn't have liked it. He didn't like it himself for different reasons. He passed it and studied an owl constructed out of a rusty piece of wood. Two youths with wire limbs embraced each other. On the wall there was another painting which showed a lilac room and sitting on the floor in front of a long mirror either a chimpanzee or an ape. One picture in particular fascinated him. It showed a small shadow in the foreground and another larger one behind it as if it were tracking it and were about to devour it. The shadows both had jagged outlines like black stars. He looked past the larger one to see if there was another one but there wasn't and this made him uneasy if not disappointed. The pursuing shadow was menacing and smug at the same time : he wondered if the smaller shadow was meant to be aware of the existence of the larger one, but couldn't make up his mind whether it was or not. He looked at an assortment of other paintings—one which showed a man standing with a book in his hand while behind him there brooded an image which appeared to represent Death —but always he came back to the shadows.

There was no one in the room except himself and a young man with a wispy beard who was sitting staring at a painting of velvety reds and greens : it looked like a MacTaggart, there was a deep dazzling shine about it such as one gets in stained glass windows. For the rest, there were the usual boats and hills and seas and professors and ministers and the artist's daughter and/or wife and/or dog.

After a while he left the room he was in and took a stroll round the museum which was also part of the gallery. There were replicas of ships and steam engines and boilers : there were ships becalmed in bottles, their tiny sails set for whatever stationary destinations they were headed for.

And in one section there were glass fossils, old stones, fish and coins. He studied some of the shellfish and read what was written below them, he had a look at the coins, some small and beaten and grey. And it was then that he saw her.

She was standing by a glass case staring down at one of the stones, a large grey stone such as one might find down at the seashore. And for a moment as he stood there—she was unaware of him—he imagined a timeless shore on which she was standing looking out over the briny water as if fixed in another time, far earlier than the present. Her face was quite pale and thin, she wore a brown coat with a brown hood drawn over her head. She was quite slim and she seemed to have been standing there for a long time. She wasn't beautiful at all, she merely looked thoughtful and distant and vulnerable. It was difficult to say what she was thinking of as she stared at the stone. Slung over her arm was a brown handbag the colour of her coat. Her eyes he couldn't see

26

but he imagined that they were also brown. She looked about twenty-six but her figure was girlish and exquisitely defenceless.

"They're quite old," he said casually as he stood beside her.

"Yes," she said in a slightly startled way as if she were emerging out of a dream. "Yes, they're old and beautiful."

He wondered what Dixon would have said at that particular moment to retain her interest and keep her talking.

He said, "They look quite blank."

"Yes," she said with some animation, "that is exactly how they look, quite blank."

"Do you visit museums often?" he said carefully. "I must say that I find them interesting myself. Lots of people don't bother." He thought his voice sounded priggish, a bit like Dixon, with the implication that he himself was slightly superior to other people. He found it hard to say anything that didn't sound artificial, as if the words would hang in the air after he had spoken them.

"Sometimes," she said. "Sometimes on a Sunday. But I must be . . ." She looked quickly at a very small silvery wrist-watch and turned away. He could not think of anything at all to say which would hold her there. It was galling to see her go when his book needed her but he wasn't quick-thinking enough to make smart or chatty conversation.

Dixon needed her : why couldn't he think of something to say? Dixon might show off his knowledge of stones (Dixon had read such a lot) but neither Dixon nor he could think of anything. He stood there tongue-tied watching her go out the door.

"Goodbye," she said in a fluttery manner. He noticed that the ringlets of hair below the hood were brown and that the inside of the hood was of some whitish stuff, probably angora.

"Bugger it," he thought, as he saw her leaving. "Dixon's on his own now." His first attempt hadn't been very successful. But then Dixon was a bit inhibited : that was why he had left his wife, or his wife had left him. He wondered if Dixon would believe in fate, in the stars, and decided that he wouldn't. Well, Dixon would have to stay for a bit longer in his flat and do without her; perhaps someone else would turn up. He went down the steps staring at the woman with hatred. There was no sign of the girl. Perhaps she had a car, though he couldn't remember hearing one leave. He felt suddenly desolated and angry with Dixon for being so stupid. Now he wouldn't be able to proceed with his book.

He walked along the street between the trees as if he expected the girl to appear at the end of the avenue like Garbo departing to a discreet music at the end of a film. "Damn, damn, damn," he muttered. He looked up at the windows as if he could see Dixon waiting there. Perhaps Dixon was blaming him for not getting the girl. He could imagine Dixon turning away from his book and lighting another cigarette. It would be a boring evening for him as well. He felt in a strange way responsible for Dixon. He turned into a pub and ordered a lager. He would have to be careful as he didn't want to spend too much of his saved money. He reckoned he had enough to live on for about three months. Gathering the long skirts of his khaki coat about him he sat down in a corner by himself and watched dispiritedly the antics of a third-rate comedian on the coloured TV. The colours seemed garish and vulgar after the paintings he had seen, and he was reminded that Dixon wouldn't possibly come to such a pub to drink : he wondered if in fact there was any pub in the area which Dixon would patronise, outside the lounges of hotels. Damn him, anyway, why hadn't he been able to say anything interesting to the girl? For some reason her thin pale face rising out of the collar of the brown coat and surmounted by the hood haunted him. He might even have taken her to the pictures if it had been up to him.

He couldn't hear a word of what was being said on the TV owing to the roar of conversation around him, two men in particular with their arms lovingly around each other singing *Auld Lang Syne.* How natural they were! How the tears sprang unbidden to their eyes as they dreamed of some lost world which they had once inhabited, probably some slum in the city. At any rate they were lost in the moment, surrendered to it, poured into it as water into a vase, swaying together, arms round each other, their unshaven faces lit by a distant romantic glow. Damn you, Dixon, he thought, why don't you leave me alone? Why don't you go back to your study?

4

THE FOLLOWING DAY there was a ring at Tom's doorbell (the only one of the two bells that actually worked) and Seumas Crawford came in. Tom could never understand why Seumas took it into his head to visit him now and again. Was it because he genuinely thought that he had a future as a writer or was it simply that he had nowhere else to go at those particular times? They had been in the same class many years before, but Seumas was now a university lecturer which represented some sort of success, and certainly a reasonable amount of money. It wasn't a particularly good university but it wasn't a terribly bad one either. Sometimes Tom envied Seumas, at other times he was appalled by him.

Seumas wore a red velvet jacket and had bright curly hair : he looked like a flawed and slightly girlish Renaissance man; sometimes he reminded Tom of a youth he had seen in a painting lounging against a tree with a field of flowers all round him. He quite liked Seumas but he knew that he didn't know anything of life. He had left school, gone to university and had stayed at university. His whole life had been involved in education. He was a bookish aesthete. And Tom didn't think that he was particularly bright.

"May I see it?" said Seumas, glancing at a rumpled page which Tom had thrown from the typewriter in a fever of inspiration and which was drifting in the draught which came in under the door. Bars of cold sunlight lay across the dulled flowery carpet.

"I should prefer not," said Tom. He really didn't like other people looking at his work before he had finished. It was like someone touching the hem of his garment and taking some of the virtue from him. That was why he liked staying where he stayed. No one in the building could be accused of knowing anything about the arts. Below him there stayed an old man who lived by himself and had a large dog which snapped at him whenever he took it out for a walk. Tom thought this rather odd, that this man had this dog for years and yet he looked untamed, baring his teeth and snapping at his master when he took him out. He never actually bit him but looked as if he might. Very odd that. Still he supposed that everyone had to have some being to which he must connect, on however minimal a leash. The only trouble was that the dog looked really fierce and dishevelled and he barked continually which made him appear more dangerous and menacing.

"Whatever you say," said Seumas. But he looked so disappointed that Tom immediately relented. "Oh, all right," he said, but he felt at the same time that he had betrayed something in himself and that life was composed of these little betrayals, not major ones. "I couldn't care less. It's not important anyway."

Seumas unfolded the crinkled page and read it as best he could since the typing wasn't very professional.

It read as follows :

One day at about three o'clock Dixon entered the Art Museum and stood there gazing at the paintings. There were not many that he liked really. They all looked very strange and odd and even malevolent, some of people with little heads like berries, some showing strange rooms with men crouched in corners in lilac paint. As he stood there—he had come in

*the first place because he was bored of his flat already and
he couldn't get going on his book—he saw standing by a glass
case full of stones a young girl wearing a hood and a coat.
She was holding one of the stones in her hands: she looked
very remote. She reminded him of someone but he couldn't
think who. He decided to talk to her because there was no
one else there. And he also felt alone. What he wanted above
all was someone to talk to. Sunday was a terrible day. In
any case this was the only place open on a Sunday, this Art
Gallery. He wanted to say something brilliant to her so that
she would immediately recognise his quality. He was afraid
of telling her his name because she might not have heard of
him, though she looked educated. Something about her, some
deep pathos, attracted him. It was partly to do with her
profile and the line of her back. It made her look like a lady
in a pre-Raphaelite painting. She looked defenceless and at
the same time she looked interesting. He . . .*

"I stopped there," said Tom, "because I couldn't get any
further."

"Hm. A bit repetitious, I'd say," said Seumas. "Have you
ever read the account of the meeting in *Anna Karenina*?
That is how to handle things, I think."

Seumas was one of those lecturers who have no idea how to
evaluate literature and are therefore continually comparing
passages from one book with passages from another book. He
had no qualms about comparing, for instance, the scene in
the cave in *A Passage to India* with that in *Kidnapped* and
pointing out significant parallels, not even omitting to mention the difference in the physical appearances with regard
to the different areas inside which they were located. The
death of a consumptive in Tolstoy he would compare with
the death of Little Nell in Dickens, and point out linguistic

32

• •

parallels and "echoes", quite unconscious of the fact that the first had originally been written in Russian. He would write and say things like, "What precisely we have here is the beginning of a trend in the work of Sherwood Anderson." Every author became for him in the end the equal of every other author and his main occupation in life was to find, if he could, parallels in scenes, sentences, paragraphs. He was like a cartographer tracing strata, rifts, canyons in a wholly undifferentiated landscape. He would write monographs with titles like *The Use of Painting in Stevens and Oscar Wilde*. He drew attention to the image of the castle in both Kafka and the Arthurian Legends. He didn't really believe that Kafka had actually read the Arthurian legends: rather he seemed to think that there was a common stuff of which all books, no matter what their date in history, consisted. It was difficult to dislike him because he was always so enthusiastic and so innocent.

"Hm," he said, "a bit like Malamud or Bellow, I would say. Something about the sentences. Some way in which they move carelessly without art and yet with art. I would say something urban."

"Would you like a cup of tea?" said Tom because he didn't have any beer and he couldn't understand how anybody could talk like that.

"No, thanks. I thought I might drag you out. I'm due to give a talk on Sunday. I thought you might like to come. And we could have a drink."

For the thousandth time Tom wondered why Seumas bothered to visit him. Was he really a failure like himself? Did the others in the department despise him? Or did he really think that Tom was going to write something good and did he perhaps feel that he ought to be in on it from the beginning?

33

Or was Tom the only person who would listen to him? Tom always looked on him as on a child. How would he have done at that labouring job for instance in the islands that summer? Not very well presumably. Or that road-making job?

"What are you talking about?" he asked.

"Oh, The Novel as a matter of fact. I thought I would talk about The Novel. I think you might be interested. It's a group of teachers. It will pass an afternoon for you. They are usually good audiences. Very polite."

Or was it that Tom was a reminder of his past when he had been a star pupil in that crummy school, the dux who did so well in the bursary Competition so that they had got a half holiday out of it those many years ago? He could still remember the waving of bags, the cheering. For a moment he felt a certain pathos as he looked at this perennially youthful figure, whose main work in life was to draw parallels across a map of literary stuff, and sensed something tragic there. The eyes looked tired and baggy and the bright clothes a gay façade behind which there was overwhelming boredom and failure. The lecture would almost certainly be terrible, awful, hellish, dull, like a PhD thesis. But he might get a drink out of it and on the other hand Dixon had again ground to a full stop. Nothing could be done about him for a long time. He was sure that Dixon would not know anyone like Crawford anyway. Not people with shallow minds, with this mishmash of stuff in their pointed heads.

He thought: Perhaps I'll never get this novel—but he stopped there. One must never even think things like that. For if he didn't write, what could he do? Become a postman, a labourer, an assistant manager in a third-rate hotel? Become a—

No, he felt that he could write. It was just that there was

a bluntness that he would have to overcome. He would have to arrive at an easy artifice. He would have to believe strongly enough in the world of make-believe. Behind him he felt the ironic gaze of Dixon, precisely watching him, like a fixed star.

"Yes," he said, "I'll go. Have you your car? Will you call for me?"

"Of course," said Seumas. He was very fond of his car, very precise about its performances. He drove carefully and read all the books on the handling of cars. He was terrified lest some day he should have an accident, though not because of physical fear but rather because of proved inefficiency in the "real world". Having an accident in a car was not exactly the same as making a wrong judgment on a writer, even a dead one. He had simply never connected the two worlds. Since he had bought the car he had tracked down many references to cars in literature and had got hooked for a time on the works of Scott Fitzgerald which had in turn led to comparisons between the loner in *The Great Gatsby* and the tradition of the Cowboy in American literature. He was meditating a brief pamphlet on the artists and writers who had been killed in car crashes, including Camus and Pollock. He thought an analogy could be established between the blurred canvases of action painting and the world of "reality" seen from a car travelling at high speed.

Tom was practically the only person he could talk to. He didn't like the people in his department, feeling that they were frivolous and inadequately informed and dangerously open to the poisonous effluvium of the pop world. They never kept up with the latest American critical books. They made intuitive simplistic judgments. He partly looked on Tom as someone he might rescue. Consider that life he led, alone in his flat, doing odd jobs now and again, wearing that silly

35

smelly old khaki coat. (Did he look on himself as some sort of metaphysical soldier? There was something in Wallace Stevens about that.) There was an admirable strength about his single-mindedness. Not that he was a good writer, at least as yet, but at the same time there was a moral weight about him. Still there had been that little poem he had shown him once. That had been quite nice. Influenced certainly by Williams (*The Wheelbarrow* in fact it had been called) but still interesting.

Perhaps there was a slim hope that Tom might in fact emerge some day as a discovery and he himself might write a little preface to his work. There was always that possibility.

He left with the knowledge that Tom at last would be in the audience for his talk.

After he had gone Tom went back to his typewriter. However, he was destined to be interrupted again.

There was a ring at the doorbell and when he answered it, it was the woman from across the landing with a jar of jam.

Her name was Mrs Harrow and she was a small, dark, bespectacled, dynamic woman who had been divorced, as she had told him once, from her husband who worked in a bar. She had one son who never came to visit her but had cleared off north one day with his guitar, his clothes, and all the money he could find in the house.

"I thought I'd bring you some jam," she said. She never came into the flat and he had never invited her in, except once or twice when he had come to the flat at the beginning she had somehow managed to enter under some pretext that he couldn't remember.

She seemed to be convinced that he was starving and that her mission in life was to act like an emissary from Oxfam, bringing him gifts of shortbread, scones and jam at fairly regular intervals.

36

She would sometimes say to him, "I heard you typing till all hours last night," though for such a statement to be true she would have had to have supernatural hearing since he couldn't imagine anyone hearing him typing from across the landing.

"Thank you very much," he said, holding the jar carefully. He hardly ever ate any jam. Sometimes he would buy a loaf and throw it out without touching it. He had no refrigerator and milk went sour on him. The cupboard was often full of rotten apples and oranges. At times he would find himself inexplicably short of tea and sugar.

For lack of something to say he asked, "How is your house going?" She said she had bought a big flat with nine rooms which she intended to use for taking in lodgers, preferably students.

"I'm wallpapering it," she said, "at the moment."

"You're doing it all yourself?" he said, trying to inject some enthusiasm into his voice.

"And painting it," she said. "I'm hoping to get some students. I'll sell this place of course when it's finished."

He had the feeling that she couldn't succeed in her project, that it was merely a dream, and that she wasn't businesslike enough to keep the flat going. Sometimes in fact he wondered whether it was not all a fantasy, and that she didn't have this flat at all. After all, where did she get the money from? He had heard that she had been a receptionist in a hotel for many years, and receptionists weren't highly paid.

"I'll have to buy some furniture," she added. She had already told him that she would get most of the furniture cheap at sales. He imagined vast rooms furnished with different kinds of chairs and tables like the detritus of an insane mind, and students sitting about on antique beds studying philosophy. He thought of her busily scouring the

37

city for wardrobes and sideboards. "I shall paint one of the bedrooms green," she said. "Green is such a restful colour. I shall have to do the painting myself. Painters are so expensive."

She had a fixed idea that if she got students the tone of the establishment would be automatically raised and it would become elegant and chic. He could have told her that she might have difficulty in getting money from students. Also that they might be very noisy.

She was really a very odd person. Every morning she would leave the house in her brown fur coat which looked as if it had been bitten by nocturnal animals, and return in the late afternoon. Perhaps she had been wallpapering her house. Or perhaps there was no house at all. In that case he couldn't imagine how she was spending her time.

"I could pay all of it off, in ten years," she said. "My bank manager told me." She said this as if she owned the bank manager.

"What are you working at now?" she asked him shyly.

"Nothing much," he replied.

He was convinced that she would tell her friends—if she had any—that there was a famous author living near her and that he spent his time typing furiously in the pursuit of masterpieces.

"Of course," he could imagine her saying, "the house is in one of the better quarters of the city."

He wondered what she would do if he volunteered to help her with her painting and wallpapering and for a moment he nearly did.

"Well, I hope you like the jam," she finally said, half turning away. He thought, perhaps Dixon would stay in her house, perhaps he could become one of her lodgers, perhaps he would fall in love with her. Now that would be an idea.

38

Dixon wouldn't like her, he was sure. Especially if there were students. But the image was very strong, of Dixon writing busily in one of her rooms, while she tiptoed about in a devout silence, and made tea for him and told him of her life, of "reality". The image was so strong that for a moment he forgot that she was real and Dixon imaginary.

"Well," he said again, "thank you for the jam."

"I suppose you'll have to get on with your work," she said.

"I'm afraid so," he said with an assumed pathos as if he were an Atlas of literature.

"Well, make sure you take your food," she said. "One of these days I'll bring you some home-made oatcakes."

"Thank you," he said, again assuming his small-boy voice.

"Well . . ." She turned away.

"And I hope you'll get your wallpapering done all right," he added.

"Oh, don't worry about that," she said. "I'll have no bother with that. I'll have it ready in the summer."

This time she left and went into her own flat. He retired into his room, looked for a considerable time at his typewriter, and decided that he wouldn't do any more writing. He put the jam jar in the cupboard and promptly forgot all about it. Then he switched on the TV.

But he couldn't settle to watch the programme. He couldn't get the image of Dixon out of his mind. Where was he at that precise moment? What had he done to himself? He imagined him leaving his house and settling in at a flat, carrying with him his typewriter and going back furtively for some of his books. He would certainly need his books. They would all belong to the eighteenth century, epigrammatic and formal. Montesquieu would be one of the authors. The trouble was that he himself hadn't read Montesquieu. In fact, when he thought about it, it was difficult for him to get into Dixon's mind. Perhaps Dixon wouldn't be able to write at all. Perhaps he needed the abrasiveness of his wife. Perhaps without her he would die. He would certainly have to meet this girl. Mrs Harrow wouldn't do. Mrs Harrow was the type of woman who had probably destroyed her own happiness by ambition : her lowly station was not enough for her. She would dream at night of owning a hotel and not merely serving in one.

Perhaps that would be her next fantasy. He thought, Really, I must see if this house of hers exists. He felt that this was important. It would be good if it existed, it would be a guarantee of something. On the other hand if it didn't exist he would feel disappointed. It didn't matter whether it was suitable for Dixon or not; certainly she wouldn't be suitable for Dixon. Not with all her students and her bourgeois ideas. Dixon would be terrified by her rows of *Reader's Digest*; he was absolutely sure that she would have such books. She was exactly the type who would know more about Dornford Yates than about W. B. Yeats. He imagined a crazy conversation between her and Dixon in which this confusion mystified them. He burst out laughing and then suddenly stopped. He got up and began to make some tea.

5

WHEN TOM SPENCE was in school an imaginative teacher had dubbed him "Emily Brontë" because of his habit of slouching along the street by himself with a peculiar loping stride. He didn't mix very much with other pupils and he wasn't very clever. He was the only son of a small, bald, worried bank clerk and his huge rather overwhelming wife. She had wanted her husband "to get on in the world" but he hadn't succeeded owing to the fact that he was a great reader of books, many of which were beyond his mental capacity to digest. His wife on the other hand never read any books at all and did her best to stop her husband "from wasting his time". The dreadful story of her life was that she was always being ignored because her husband was a "nobody". At the annual staff party no one ever spoke to her though she wanted to be the queen there, forgetting or not realising that she had no qualities to make her queen anywhere. For this reason she blamed her husband, and their nights consisted of long silences punctuated not exactly by quarrels (since he didn't say much) but by long monologues on her part. She had a habit too of taking to her bed with strange illnesses and deciding that she wouldn't cook any meals.

Eventually her husband retired to a shed in the garden and in summer months he would sit there and take notes. He steadily read his way through the Russian novelists that he got through the post after joining a book club. After that he read the whole of Dickens and Somerset Maugham. He felt guilty if he was not reading a book: reading was a secret vice like taking heroin. He kept a large red notebook in which he entered the titles of all the books he had read, with notes on each. His note on *War and Peace* read as follows:

The action of this book takes place in Russia during the time of Napoleon. A lot of it is said to be autobiographical. This is reputed to be the greatest novel ever written. Tolstoy became very religious and is said to have made his own shoes.

His greatest luxury was to sit in a deckchair among the humming of bees reading very slowly page after page of a good book.

When Tom Spence was in school his mother expected that he would be an outstanding success. She would often visit the school complaining that her son was not getting enough homework. She didn't understand much of what he was doing, but did notice once that he had misspelt one of the words she knew and wrote in to mention it. She kept in the sideboard all the letters she had received from the school (they were all written on school notepaper) and she would show them to any visitors she had. The result of this of course was that her son was not liked by the masters, who found him surly and inclined to overrate himself for no apparent reason.

At the age of eight he began to suffer from bouts of bronchitis which slowed him down even further. His mother would keep him in bed for three weeks or so and sometimes would take him into her own bed. He breathed with difficulty, and it wasn't until years afterwards that he recognised that this was because of the overwhelming personality of his mother who was squeezing the life out of him while she plagued the doctor with threats and demands. In the summer months he would lie in bed eating oranges while outside on the street he could hear the other children happily playing and shouting.

In self-defence he began to withdraw into himself like his father, and would read poetry. His favourite poets were Kipling and Alfred Noyes. In the dead of night he would lie awake staring lifelessly at the window through which the moonlight poured, while his mother snored beside him.

As time passed she realised that he was not going to be her saviour. His arithmetic or what she called sums was bad. His French and Latin were worse. He himself had grown cynical about school. He would take days off and she wouldn't find out about it for weeks. He would go away by himself down streets he had never visited before, wander among barrows of vegetables and fruit, sit and watch the trains leave the railway station. He began to read travel books. In fact the only thing that caught his fancy in school was a project they once did on Greece. He decided that when he was older he would go there. There was lots of sunshine and plenty of fine marble statues that weren't able to talk.

One day his father didn't come back into the house from the shed. They found him lying slumped over a copy of *Pygmalion*. He had just begun to write his opinion of it when the pen fell to the floor. The only words written there were :

The background to this play is said to be a Greek legend. The use of the phrase "not bloody likely" caused a com- motion in the theatre. Higgins is said to be Shaw since he wrote postcards to people rather than letters.

Later Tom counted the number of entries in the notebook. There were two hundred. There were also fifteen other notebooks with similar entries. He didn't know very much about his father, who hardly spoke to him at all in his latter days. His face had settled into an expression of perpetual puzzlement and it was almost as if he had to be pushed from one assignment to another.

His mother bought a large black veil, but there weren't any mourners at the funeral which took place in a large, draughty cemetery. She kept the letter from the bank manager who had arrived briefly in a large blue car and had then driven off to take his boat out for the afternoon. The name of his boat was the *Interest*, a pleasant little joke that had floated into his mind when he was having a bath one Sunday afternoon.

At the age of seventeen Tom left the house. He didn't even leave a note. He had taken a number of his father's books —the more modern ones—and his father's pen. His mother had kept up for some time the fiction that he had gone to England to train as a bank manager to follow in his father's footsteps, but eventually the neighbourhood discovered that he had been seen working as a labourer and later still that he had been seen delivering parcels at Christmas. After that she had tired of keeping up the pretence and Tom had heard that she had taken up with another small man exactly like her husband who worked as a joiner in a yard. They would be seen on Saturday nights in a local bar called the Royal and she seemed quite happy. She took to wearing flamboyant colours but when drunk she would refer to "happier days" when her "brilliant" son had been thwarted by bronchitis and consumption. She would even show people the notebooks which her "brilliant" bank manager husband had compiled in his leisure hours and had once been introduced on the strength of them to a schoolmaster who had said that they were "remarkable".

Tom's odyssey had begun in the West where he had helped to build a road with a number of mainly Irish labourers in beautiful summer weather which had lasted for weeks. On Sundays he would go for endless walks across the heathery moors and brood by lochs till the sun began to set. It was on one of those evenings that two or three lines of poetry had come into his head. When he got back he wrote them down in a writing pad. However, when the rains came he decided that he would leave the road-building and go back to the city, where he got a job for a while helping in a bar. He began to save his money so that he could take time off to write. He also began to read some of his father's books and though he found them difficult he persevered because there was nothing else for him to do. The first two weeks he managed to stay off work he had written nothing at all except a very short poem which he had sent away and which had been returned. In those days he was in digs with a Mrs Thin who wanted only the "companionship" (as she was quite old) and wasn't really interested so much in the money. She was frightened of burglars and also had a fantasy that gangs were stealing her milk. Eventually he found the smell of Mansion Polish unbearable and left. For a small deposit he discovered that he could buy a flat, and moved in one spring day with his books and nothing much else. One day when he was looking out of the window at the river which flowed past in the distance the idea of writing a book about another writer had come to him. It had come to him purely as a gift, unsolicited yet transparent, and he had started work on the book.

When he started the book on Dixon he had been reading Hermann Hesse in paperback. He spent his time either

45

reading, or watching TV, or walking about. He had no friends at all, believing that if he was going to write he must lead a life of self-sacrifice and loneliness. Sometimes when he could afford it he went to the cinema. He found that his main difficulty was to write something that he himself felt, for when he reread pages of his work he seemed to hear Hesse or someone like him speaking through them. But at the same time writing was all that he could do even minimally well. Sometimes he had terrible nightmares as he walked through the city of being swallowed by a huge organism which glittered with vulgar lights. And he knew that he must learn to breathe properly before it succeeded. He grew sensitive to colour : the saddest sight he knew was the milky neon lamps glowing against the fading daylight before they slowly turned to orange. The happiest was the colours of apples and oranges and tomatoes on a fruit stall on a spring day.

He had given himself four years "to succeed" as a writer though he hadn't defined what success meant. He knew no writers except for a few poets, inadequately bearded, whom he had heard reading some concrete poems in a poky pub. They all said before they began reading, "This is a thing that I wrote . . ." They used the word "shit" a lot : he didn't like that; it was unnecessary. It was unrefined. All he wanted to do was to write one really good thing. He thought that their work was trivial and pretentious, he was certain that their talent was minimal; and he conjectured that they were massive egotists. They dressed like disciples—indeed there was something of the New Testament in their style—and they tried desperately hard to make their conversation intelligent. He didn't want to be like them. No, it would be far better to be large and sane like Tolstoy.

He didn't know what he would do when the four years were up and he hadn't "succeeded". Anyway he still had a year and a half to go. He didn't have enough certificates to take him into a university. There seemed not very much open to him. Though he supposed that he was still young enough to go to night school and try for more certificates. He could probably do that if the worst came to the worst. But on the other hand he must try and finish his novel. He would have a real go at it. The thing was not to be afraid, to live sparely as Dixon would do. To remember that Art must be worked for.

6

THE GROUP WHICH Crawford was to address seemed
to consist of school teachers; at least there was a disciplined
receptivity about them and much flashing of spectacles and
notebooks. Tom sat at the back trying to appear inconspicu-
ous, for everyone about him seemed neatly suited or quietly
bloused. There appeared to be more women than men and
they maintained a decorous silence as if they were in
church.

After a while Crawford appeared and sat modestly in front
of a table on which there rested a carafe of water with a glass
beside it. An oldish man with a grey moustache introduced
him as their "speaker for this afternoon" and said that he
was sure that they would have a stimulating hour as Mr
Crawford was a lecturer who had composed many interesting
papers. He added that he was a PhD. The theme of The
Novel had been suggested by the committee as suitable for
those who were teaching senior classes and they all knew the
difficulty some of them had with the prose section of the
Higher Certificate. And this reminded him of a little joke.
After he had told the joke there was a comfortable decorous
laughter. Then after a final eulogy of Mr Crawford as one
of the "new minds" he sat down.

Crawford stood up and began by saying how much he
was overawed by the subject he had undertaken to talk
about. The novel was indeed an immense field of study,
though in fact its genesis was relatively recent. The novel
presented many problems to a speaker. One of the problems

was that there were different kinds of novels. There was for instance *Ulysses* and there was *Tom Jones*. It was arguable that *The Canterbury Tales* was a novel in verse.

What then was a novel? He suggested that first of all the novel was a structure (usually fairly long, though not always) which had characters, though not necessarily a paraphrasable plot. It was normally written in prose. Was *Finnegan's Wake* a novel? He thought that it was though it was a different novel from, say, the novels of the nineteenth century.

The novel had arisen at the time of the rise of the middle classes. However, one must be clear about one thing, there were novels in Elizabethan times though in those days the novel was not the dominant form. In Elizabethan times the play and the poem were the dominant forms. Shakespeare had never written a novel, though if he had lived in the nineteenth century it was almost certain that he would have been a novelist. He might in fact have been the Dickens of the novel for there were many resemblances between the two writers. For instance there were characters in Dickens and Shakespeare which blurred the line between comedy and tragedy. He himself for instance believed that there were many resemblances between Scrooge and Shylock. And then of course there was *Robinson Crusoe* which dealt with the ethics of capitalism. There again was a book which was called a novel though for most of the time the stage was inhabited by only one man. (The entrance of Man Friday introduced the exploited man as one got him in the works of Cooper and later writers. It could be argued that the cannibal scene was an ironic scenario for precisely the "red in tooth and claw" nature of capitalism.)

Tom's attention wandered to the window which was beside him and to the scenes which it framed. A drunk who had presumably come out of a house (since hotels and bars

49

were shut at that time of day) was engaged in coiling himself round a lamp-post with a totally serious look on his face while he muttered some words to himself. Now and again he would raise himself up to an upright posture and say something to a passer-by, his slack grey unshaven face assuming momently different expressions, from aggression to empty hopelessness. Further on past the drunk he could see a girl in a stained yellow dress skipping endlessly with a rope, her pigtails dancing up and down her back. Directly in front of him he could see the mutilated name of a shop. It said, "GR H M MEN O TF TTER". At a corner a red-haired boy was standing selling papers.

He turned his attention back to the speaker who was saying: "... about the novel is the position of the narrator. This I find the most interesting thing of all. In most novels of course the narrator pretends that he is God. One could argue that the universe itself is a structure or a novel of which God is the ultimate narrator." Tom noticed a little grey-haired woman taking all this down in a notebook, head bent. "And indeed it might be what science fiction writers are doing. The issue of science fiction raises further questions which it might not be in our interest to pursue. I should however point to an exemplar like Blish, some of whose works you may have read."

When Tom looked again the drunk had disappeared. Instead he could see two women talking to each other. One who was fat stood squatly in front of the other one who wore a red hat and was gesticulating freely with her right hand. Her back was to him and he speculated as to whether she was an Italian. As he watched, he heard the sound of music and then there came into his space of observation a Salvation Army band marching along and singing *Onward Christian Soldiers*. They looked quite military : the man at the front

of the column seemed lost in a dream of generalship while
the pale bespectacled women also marched with a fine pride
and hauteur. Why did the ugliest girls attend poetry readings
and join choirs, he wondered?

Crawford was saying: "... But of course if one is a
Marxist and one also reads novels one arrives at the interesting question : will the narrator always give the point of view
of the class to which he belongs? And there are other questions which arise. Will the narrator leave out things which he
doesn't want to put in? Does the narrator play fair? Who is
the narrator? What age is he? Where does he come from?
Is he himself an artist? What is the relationship between the
narrator and the novelist himself? Do they both come from
the same class? Is the narrator to be considered as a
historian? That is, a historian of fiction. And what is fiction?
Is everything fiction really? Wallace Stevens might have said
that. From the point of view of an unseen reality is everything fiction? Is not only the narrator fictitious but the
novelist himself? Which leads us to ideas of order and dis-
order. Is the novel an attempt to impose order? How much
of what he does is the novelist himself aware of? The
questions proliferate. Though the novelist pretends that he
is not the narrator how can this be? Who is the narrator of
Kafka's novels, the mysterious K? Indeed are they novels
at all? I am talking here of novels told in the first person,
of course, but there are also novels which are not told in
the first person. Indeed most novels are not told in the first
person. In which case is the hero the novelist himself in
disguise? One is led here along the endless avenues of
Freud. And then one might well ask : Is every structure a
novel? Is every story—and remember that the word story is
the same word as we get in history—is every story a novel?
One has to remember for instance that science is a relatively

recent phenomenon and the demand for proof, for objective proof, is also very recent."

When he looked out the window again Tom saw a woman trying to back her car out from between two others. Her face showed concentration and panic in varying degrees, her gloves clamped tight on the wheel. He wondered what was going on in her mind. Was she perhaps married and thinking that her husband would laugh at or be angry with her if anything happened to the car? She must of course be aware of the passers-by. Did the pressure of their stare make her feel incompetent? He had the curious feeling of eavesdropping (if that was the word) on a mind nakedly in trouble but he could not draw his eyes away. The face seemed to be looking inward though the eyes were on the road, for at that moment the road was everything, the road was the whole world. It was where she had come to with all the equipment of emotion she had gathered throughout her whole life. She pulled the car round without touching the bumper of the car behind her. Eventually she got out on to the road and he could see her visibly relaxing. She had accomplished something, it would be part of her life.

"... the crucial question, the relationship of the novelist to his characters. Does the novelist approve of his characters? Does he admire them? Does he hate them? Is he indifferent to them? In the latter case of course he won't be a good novelist. Is he unfair to them? (Was Shakespeare unfair to Shylock?) What does go on in the process of creation? We know that novelists and scientists are very like each other when they make their great discoveries. And there are questions of identity. A novelist may choose irony as a weapon. A novelist may be autobiographical. Where do the novelist's characters come from? One must argue that they come from

52

experience or from his reading or from a combination of both."

At that moment quite by chance Tom saw her. For some reason she turned round and there she was sitting about six rows in front of him, the girl he had met in the Art Gallery. And at that moment he knew that Dixon was predestined to be saved. He knew it by pure intuition. It was coincidence in real life. If Crawford hadn't come to see him, if they hadn't been at school together, if he himself hadn't decided to come and listen to the talk, then he wouldn't have seen her. It was fated. Crawford himself had a hand in the novel, he had a part to play. She hadn't even seen him or if she had seen him she hadn't recognised him, but she was his prey. She had become print in front of his eyes, sentences, paragraphs. This time he wouldn't let her go. He waited impatiently for Crawford to finish.

". . . predestined or spontaneous, that is the real question. Isn't it? That is to say, does the novelist exert complete control over his characters so that he may be considered a Calvinist, or does he give them freedom of the will such that he is a generous God? That is the question. If we had the time we might go more deeply into this question, applying it to various novelists. I myself would put Dickens in the latter class. And perhaps Hawthorne into the former class. However I have merely been propounding theories. I hope that you will yourselves speculate on what I have said."

He sat down to applause and the man with the grey moustache stood up and asked for questions. There was a long silence interrupted at last by a woman who stood up with a notebook in her hand.

"I should like to ask Mr Crawford," she said, "what he thinks of permissiveness in the modern novel."

Tom looked at her in amazement. Where had she been for

the past hour? There had been poor Crawford disquisiting, or whatever the word was, on philosophical aspects of the novel in his random way and this was all she could ask. For a moment he felt sympathy for Crawford as he stood up and began to improvise an answer using the time-honoured opening words, "It depends what you mean by 'modern novel'. If you mean Kafka . . ." Christ, thought Tom, doesn't he know that she doesn't mean Kafka? That she's never heard of Kafka? What's the use? What's the use of it all?

When Crawford had sat down another man got up and said, "That may be very well but we all know—" he turned round and looked at the people behind him in the manner of the practised orator—"we all know, that is all of us who have the well-being of the young at heart, that our bookstalls are loaded with filth. Only the other day a parent came up to me and said, 'Do you realise that that play you have given my child has words in it and expressions that are obscene?' And what could I say to her? The fact is that modern art and writing are full of filth and there is no use disguising it by talking about Kafka. How many people read Kafka? We have to be practical."

And so it went on, while more and more inexorably Crawford's defences were bludgeoned from angles which he had not expected. Perhaps he was longing for irony to defend himself with but how much irony is there around on a Sunday afternoon? The final question was: "Should we read novels with children in the class or should they take them home?"

Mercifully, the chairman looked at his watch like a harassed referee in extra time and said that there would be coffee and they were all very glad that Mr Crawford had taken the trouble to come along and give them that most interesting talk. Next week it would be Mr Tweet, talking about the "Theme of Childhood in British Literature".

Five or six women appeared with trays and the company broke up in groups and drank coffee.

Tom made his way to the girl. All around him he could hear the chatter of people released from boredom and dutiful listening. He stood for a moment and heard a woman say, "And Theresa of course who is a very advanced child said, 'But you must admit that Yeats is very boring really' and what could I say?" There was a burst of laughter. Then he saw her.

She was standing by herself with a cup of coffee in her hand. She looked exactly as she had done in the museum, self-absorbed and distant as if she were not wholly and physically in the space where she appeared to be. She wore exactly the same coat. There was a thoughtful sweetness about her which he found arresting.

"Hullo there," he said. "Remember me?"

She glanced at him in a startled way and he thought for a moment that the cup she was holding in her hand would spill.

"I'm afraid I . . ."

"The museum . . ." he said. "I met you there on . . ."

Recognition flooded her face. "Oh, of course." And then her face darkened again.

"And what are you doing here?" he asked.

"Oh, I was brought along by Mary. She stays in the same flat. She seems to have disappeared."

"Come on," he said masterfully. "This is a bore. Let's go out and get some tea somewhere."

"But," she said, "I'm already drinking tea."

"Put it away. Don't tell me that you find this interesting."

"But Mary . . . I must . . ."

"Well, tell her then." That was it, he must be masterful.

He saw her studying him wonderingly. After all he didn't look very presentable. On the other hand it might be an adventure. And certainly he had come to a talk on The Novel so he couldn't be all that barbaric, he couldn't be a ned, he would surely be safe to be with . . .

"All right," she said. He saw her talking briefly to a person whom he assumed to be her flatmate Mary and then they walked out together. He found a restaurant and they sat in a corner on the black leather seats. He ordered two coffees.

7

It was quite by chance that Dixon met her again, he wrote
that night. *One day he left his flat, overwhelmed by tedium,
and sat down on a bench in a park. It was a Sunday afternoon and there were a number of people walking up and
down, some in shirt sleeves and some not. He started to
think about painting and wished again that he were a
painter. For a painter everything was simple and almost
naive. Reality was out there in front of him. Reality didn't
have a grammatical language, soiled by moral connotations.
Oranges didn't speak: neither did apples. He thought of a*
mot: *"When an apple opens its mouth that is the danger
for a poet." He was quite pleased with this and turned it
over and over in his mind, like an opal. In fact he had often
seen opals; he had bought his wife one once.*

*The shadows of the trees composed themselves on the lawn
in front of him. Two little boys were turning cartwheels
watched by a simmering park-keeper. He looked up at the
tree in whose shadow he was sitting. The leaves, he noticed,
were turning yellow and between them he could see a bird
flying, below some white clouds. He didn't know anything
about birds though he wanted to name it. So he lowered
his gaze after a while to the slate-coloured fat pigeons in front
of him. And it was then that he saw her walking past. He
was sure it was she though she wasn't wearing the same coat.*

*He stood up suddenly and said, removing his hat,
"Haven't we met before? In the museum?" He laughed*

slightly ironically as if he were telling a joke against himself. She stopped, blushed and said, "I . . . of course . . ."

"It was last week," he said, "and you were regarding a stone. Would you care to sit down for a minute?"

She hesitated and then sat down. There was a silence for a moment and then he said, looking keenly at her and with great significance, "My name is Dixon. Drew Dixon." There was no sign of recognition on her face. He felt very disappointed but told himself, "I am sure she doesn't read novels." But it would have made things much easier if she had known his name.

"I'm Sheila," she said. "Sheila Britten."

"Aren't the pigeons lovely," he said. "So calm and peaceful. And their colours. I like their colours so much."

"They are very pretty."

"Do you come here often?" he said. "I don't know this park very well. I lived in a different part of the city."

"Quite often," she said. He noticed that she had very blue eyes, dark blue. She seemed very reposeful. She had the gift of sitting still, a very rare one.

"We seem destined to be running into each other," he said. "That's twice in a week." He listened to the phrases thinking that they sounded banal. The characters in his novels certainly didn't talk like that; he made them talk in a highly stylised manner. He recognised that his own phrases were uninteresting: he didn't know her well enough to be ironical. Anyway she was too open.

"Do you believe in predestination?" he asked, watching the park-keeper bearing down on the two boys who ran away.

"I don't know. I haven't thought of it. I don't study horoscopes. My flatmate Mary does, though."

58

"It is very warm," he said, "isn't it? I was sitting here reading a book by Hesse. Have you read him?"

"No, I'm afraid not. I'm a school teacher. I haven't much time for reading."

"Oh, you teach? Young children?"

"Yes, the young children. I am a primary school teacher. I have been teaching for seven years."

For some reason she felt wholly at ease with him. Perhaps because he had a civilised look about him. He wore a nice white hat and he carried a cane. There was a certain air of the dandy about him but he didn't look foolish, he looked composed. He spoke in a very relaxed manner. She relaxed. The trees overarching the bench gave shelter from the sun— she didn't like being too much in the hot sun, being too barely exposed—and she listened to the little children happily shouting and playing. She almost closed her eyes.

"What's over there?" her companion asked suddenly.

"Oh, that's the conservatory. They have plants there. It's very hot."

"Should you like to go and have a look at it?"

"Well..." On the other hand, why not? He seemed a pleasant enough man. "All right," she said rising to her feet. Though she was twenty-seven she had a slim figure and she looked girlish. She knew this.

They walked across the park and entered the hothouse. The heat was intense. A foreign couple dressed in large Mexican-type hats were coming out as they entered. The man waved his hands helplessly as if about to say something but perhaps he thought his English wasn't good enough. He was carrying his jacket in his hand; over his shirt he wore red braces. They walked forward into the blasting heat among the Mexican shrubs in tortured poses, cacti and other plants whose names she couldn't pronounce. It was like being in a

59

desert, in a place deprived of water and greenery; she thought that the desert didn't suit him. He looked too European for that strange nightmarish place.

When they came out he said, "Would you like an ice cream?"

Together they walked out between the wrought iron gates and entered a café.

They sat in a dark corner away from the heat of the sun and ordered ice creams. Her white dress shone in the half darkness as did his white hat. He felt daring. He couldn't remember when he had been last in a café. He would have preferred to take her to a hotel but hotels weren't open at that time. Later he might suggest it.

He cast a novelist's eye over the café. In the corner opposite there was a juke box composed of blocks of vulgar colour. He tried to find an exact parallel for it but gave up after a while. He turned back to the girl who was calmly eating ice cream. He thought, I feel almost happy, almost at peace. She is so reposeful. For a moment as she bent over her small, circular plate she reminded him of a painting by Vermeer, cool and mathematical. He wondered whether they were in the habit of washing their plates properly as he began to eat his ice cream.

8

I T T U R N E D O U T that she was a primary school teacher.
As he talked to her he wondered whether she would be suited
to Dixon. She didn't know much about literature but she
talked quite freely about the children she taught with an
endearing freshness as if they were important to her. She
would sometimes get letters and cards from them with drawings on them. Once there was a very long silence which
neither of them could fill. It wasn't that they bored each
other, it was that the two of them had come to a sudden
stop as if there was nothing in common that they could talk
about. And then she said, "What do you do then?" He told
her about his attempts to write, about his poems, about the
jobs he had had. He didn't tell her about the novel. She
wondered whether there was any money in what he was
doing. She didn't seem particularly interested in money but
it is the sort of question one asks when one has nothing
particular to say. For some reason he got angry and started
a long harangue about a materialistic society, gesticulating
freely and at one time nearly toppling her coffee cup. When
he was finished she looked at him in an amused manner and
said that it wasn't really as important as all that. Happiness
was what was important. He looked at her in amazement:
the sentiment seemed so simple and almost naive, so lacking
in contemporary sophistication, so untwisted, that he found it
almost silly. But she believed in what she was saying. He
found himself thinking of an oasis where water glittered
while around it grew the shrivelled twisted shapes of trees.

He asked her what she had thought of the lecture and she said that she had not really been interested; it wasn't her field. It was her flatmate who had wanted to come. Her flatmate wasn't really terribly interested either but she taught in a large secondary school and she thought she ought to know something about literature. As a matter of fact her flatmate—Mary—didn't read much either and spent a lot of her time listening to records. She herself didn't read much except books which she used for projects. She did a lot of that; that was what primary teaching was now about, projects. She said that the children did most of the learning themselves.

She was not at all beautiful nor even conventionally pretty. She had darkish blue eyes and a pale thinnish face and dark hair. He wasn't really very taken by her. Her mind was more practical than his but he wasn't illuminated by it. For that matter he wasn't much illuminated by his own mind. Both her parents were dead and she was used to living with her flatmate. She had been in England for a while and at one time thought of taking a job in South America but she had decided against it. The headmaster of the school was nice, she said, a man of advanced ideas. The staff were nice too. She said at one stage that he looked thin and wondered if he took enough food. No, surely, he thought, Dixon won't like her. She isn't civilised enough, fragile enough. He was sure that he wouldn't take to her at all. He wondered whether he had made a mistake. How could she be made suitable for Dixon?

But at the same time he didn't want her to leave. He was happy to see her pouring out coffee for him, it created an aura of domesticity. He didn't like coffee himself, much preferring tea. But he was wondering all the time : how could he make her suitable for Dixon? How could he change her?

Would he leave her with the same style of clothes, the same style of dress? She pointed to a woman at the next table, and said, "She shouldn't wear that hat, it doesn't suit her, she should wear navy blue." And he knew that she was quite right. But at the same time it puzzled him that she should be concerned with these quotidian things. He wasn't used to them either from his father or his mother. She glanced at the menu and said she was sure that it was too expensive. He wondered what she thought of his long khaki coat but she didn't make any comment on it. He was in fact puzzled by her. She seemed to know things that he didn't know and yet he considered the things that she knew unimportant in a deep sense. For instance, she pointed to a table mat which had a tartan motto on it and said that it was wrong. He hadn't noticed that tartan motto at all. She ought to be the novelist, he considered, she was more observant than him, he wasn't observant at all. But in point of fact he was sure that she hadn't noticed the small angels on the ceiling, with their trumpets; he had noticed them immediately. One of them had a missing wing. Perhaps it had fallen into some-one's soup.

She had a small silver watch on her wrist at which she glanced now and again.

"Look," he said at last, almost mumbling the words, "would you like to come to the cinema this week some time? I haven't been for a long time and they are showing *Shane* again. Would you like to see it? On Thursday perhaps?" He had seen the film five times already and never tired of it. There was something about the fable of the mysterious stranger coming to the rescue of the honest and lame man which appealed to a very deep part of his nature.

"Well..." She stopped and looked at him, he thought

with pity. Then after what seemed a long while she said, "All right."

He was ridiculously happy. "It's at the Regal," he told her. "You know it? It's on Regent Street."

"I'll find it," she said. And he knew she would. He had great confidence in her practical ability.

"I think I'd better pay for this," she said decisively. He wasn't at all angry and allowed her to pay, though it wasn't really very expensive. She took out a small red purse and counted out the money with a serious expression on her face. She seemed very prudent and careful. He was sure that she looked after her money like a good housewife.

At the same time he was worried that she was taking pity on him as if he were someone whom Oxfam might help, on whose behalf Christmas cards might be printed. He felt vaguely related to Barnado's Homes. And that did make him feel slightly angry. He determined that he wouldn't wear his khaki coat next time.

When she went out he looked after her through the window. He saw her trim figure walking purposefully among the people on the pavement, people he didn't know, and he watched her as a sailor might watch a ship on which he had once served with a certain sentimental wish that nothing terrible would happen to her, that in spite of everything she would outlast the storms and the treacheries of rocks. She looked quite capable of looking after herself, however, there was no question about that.

He tried to imagine a conversation between herself and Dixon and couldn't. Dixon would never have attended such a lecture anyway. He didn't quite know what Dixon would say to her but he felt that he must invent something. He felt responsible for Dixon and also responsible for her. He felt for the first time a twinge of irritation with Dixon. He ordered another coffee and stirred his spoon in it vaguely. It looked frothy and cheap and almost vulgar. She could certainly look after Dixon's flat for him. For the first time he began to think that perhaps she was too good for Dixon but he pushed the thought to the back of his mind. Perhaps on the other hand Dixon might have grown discontented with beauty and elegance. He associated her with her wristwatch, working neatly and elegantly and dependably.

He stirred his coffee insipidly. At least he would see her at *Shane* and then he would understand her better. Technically she was an orphan; the two of them at least had that in common, for though his mother might still be alive somewhere, he thought of himself as an orphan. He thought of Crawford. Poor bugger. All that guff about The Novel and all those ridiculous questions. Perhaps he should try and find him. But he didn't move from his seat. Crawford, he knew, was sure that he had done well, that his lecture had been a good one. He was incorrigible, sunny, deluded.

He rose from the table and left some money on it. He was already looking forward to the film—a combination of the old and the new—and smiling as he left the café.

3—GMD • •

9

THE GIRL'S NAME was Ann and, as she said, she
lived with a flatmate called Mary. On the death of her
mother—which occurred later than her father's—she had
concentrated exclusively on her teaching which she liked
because she got on well with children. In any case there was
nothing else that she could do. Whenever she read anything
she did so with a view to using it in a project: she hardly
ever read for pleasure. She didn't think that Tom Spence
could be a very good writer; she had in fact never met an
author before, or anyone who even said that he was an
author. She rather pitied Tom; for one thing he looked as
if he neglected himself and didn't have very much money.
That khaki coat he wore was really dreadful. There was
about him, however, a resentful, rebellious, throttled energy
which she found rather exciting. The headmaster of her
school was certainly very different. He wore conventional
clothes and was always neatly dressed. He spoke very precisely and walked about with a sunny smile. The women in
the school were also very conventional though there were
one or two interesting young ones. She sometimes wondered
whether in fact some of the older ones bored her, they were
always going on about education and "what was best for
the children" except for one waspish older one who smoked
like a furnace and said that they should be "kept in their
place". Really, however, she preferred the children, their
spontaneity, their habit of coming and telling her their secrets
openly and nakedly, their strange animal naturalness. But

otherwise she didn't meet many people, certainly not men.

She didn't know quite what to make of Tom Spence. For some reason he made her uneasy. He looked at her sometimes as if he wasn't seeing her but someone else. She had noticed this particularly and it made her feel rather eerie. She had never been looked at in that way before, with that kind of remoteness. On the other hand she thought that he was safe enough. In fact he seemed in many ways naive. She was quite sure that he hadn't seen much of the world : she herself had been to training college though not to a university. She had decided not to go to university, though she could have gone, because she wanted to earn money as soon as possible.

She was used to looking after herself. She was good at sewing and cooking. She saved a certain amount of money every month from her salary and put it in the bank. Her expenditure wasn't high though she did spend some money of her own on books and magazines for the children—there was never enough material in the school and one needed so much nowadays. It wasn't like the old days when they sat behind desks without moving and all they needed might be one or two books in a whole year. Now enormous numbers of books and magazines were necessary, massive amounts of information. The books had to be left lying about to attract them. She also bought newspapers, anything that would provide facts and data. Some nights she would spend hours looking out bits and pieces for a particular project. She ransacked libraries, made notes, listened to radio programmes. She had a small tape recorder as well as a record player.

While she made her way back to her flat she wondered why she had consented to seeing Tom Spence. Was it that she was growing bored with the people in the school? Was it that she was lonely? She didn't really have enough time to feel lonely except sometimes at the weekends. Was it that she felt the danger of becoming a typical schoolmistress, such as one might see in caricatures, with a self-satisfied childish mind? Was it that she felt a spirit of adventure stirring in her? She didn't really know much about Tom. For all she knew he might live in a slum, or he might have no place to live in at all. But the latter, she remembered, was not true; he had mentioned a flat. She couldn't imagine what the flat was like, probably very untidy. Still she didn't really believe in him as an author, though on the other hand, to be fair, that could have been said about many artists who had later become famous. And nowadays you couldn't tell from their appearance what people were like: they all looked unwashed and untidy. Her own mind was very conventional and she liked to see people dressing properly.

But she found just the same that she was looking forward to going to the cinema. It was ages since she had been: she did watch a certain amount of TV, but again that was mainly so that she could extract information for projects. She liked to watch programmes about geography and animals, and *Tomorrow's World*. But the cinema was different from TV. And the fact that he had invited her to the cinema made him safe enough. A dance hall would have been different: she might have had to think twice about that. Not that she didn't care for dancing, but nowadays there was such a lot of fighting at dances. She didn't even know where the dance halls were: her parents hadn't approved of her going to dances alone, though she was allowed to go to the school dances. But she had no romantic memories of these, for while the other girls talked of their conquests she had sat or stood about very quietly. There was no doubt, however, that she envied them, all those pink fleshy attractive girls with their mirrors and their natural hunting kit. She couldn't herself be like that and therefore there was no point in trying to be.

But if she was to go out with him she would really have to insist that he get rid of that khaki coat. He would look quite handsome in something more tidy and bright. Perhaps a red tie, a creamy shirt. He had very nice hair, curly and blonde; he could make something of that if he tried. She imagined herself refashioning him as if he were some property that belonged to her, a kind of doll whose clothing she could arrange and rearrange indefinitely. And really he must shave. She stopped at that point, half amused at herself for inventing these ridiculous plans. After all, she might choose not to go out with him after the visit to the cinema. In fact she could quite easily not turn up even for that. He would have no means of finding her again : it was purely by chance that they had met twice. Or was it? How could one tell? Perhaps it was fated. She had stopped and was looking at a jeweller's window which was packed with rings and brace- lets. They all looked very expensive and elegant and there was a very fine gold wristwatch. She had never in her whole life been given a present of jewellery by a man or boy and at that moment she felt starved as if the thought had swum into her mind for the first time. After all she was twenty- seven and not ugly. She could see her trim figure reflected in the window of the shop among the rings and she knew that she was not ugly. It was just that her personality was not spacious or confident enough : it was just that she preferred the shade, and protection.

On the other hand he himself was a bit awkward and, she was sure, quite impractical and liable to spill things and fall over things. She wasn't doing anything on that particular night anyway; she might as well go.

Tom Spence had a record player and two classical records. One was the *1812 Overture* and the other was the *Finlandia* of Sibelius. He had bought them because he thought that with their help he might bluff his way through that aspect of Dixon's personality. He thought of Dixon as a lover of classical music but he himself didn't know very much of Mozart or Beethoven or Bach, and to be truthful didn't particularly wish to explore them. His own favourite music was jazz followed closely by folk songs. He loved jazz and the more definite the beat the better he liked it. He considered it to be the greatest achievement of the twentieth century and liked the images which the music evoked in him, of cities lit by blue light, rainy streets, pianists and trumpeters in stuffy rooms. But at the same time he felt respect for Bach and Beethoven though he couldn't appreciate their music. He had a special respect for Beethoven, some of whose biographical details he had read. Something formidable and massive there, he thought, though his own feeling was for wanderers, troubadours, people who lived on their wits. He suspected that Dixon didn't like jazz: it would be altogether too smoky and primitive for him. Dixon would live among Mozartian music boxes, the elegances of the drawing room. Perhaps, however, Dixon didn't like Beethoven either, perhaps Beethoven was too stormy for him, perhaps he preferred Mozart.

Tom would play the *1812 Overture* a lot though he couldn't make up his mind whether Dixon would like it.

Still it was the only record that he had thought would be suitable at the time he bought it. He himself quite liked it though not so much as jazz or folk music. There was colour and narrative in it and he liked the skating, whirring, slightly metallic surge of the cavalry charges, etcetera. And also the sound of the anthems fighting each other to the death. *Finlandia* was different: that was slower and sadder and more leisurely. It gave an impression of empty space and dying light.

But when he had finished playing them out of a sense of duty he would play his jazz records and feel again the attraction of the spontaneous and the impromptu. The thing about jazz was that it sent your whole body dancing: classical music had very little direct impact on him. The trumpets of jazz were different from those of Tchaikovsky, there was more courage in them, individual courage, a dancing, precarious, gay courage. They emerged out of the city and loneliness and desperate traffic. They had assimilated the city and were basically joyful. Perhaps that was why he liked them so much, because he himself hadn't assimilated the city so that he could say, "My imagination is like plasticine. I can make and remake the city in any way I please."

But he also liked folk music. He liked the strange harmonies that one got, the irreverence in some of them. He liked for instance ones like *MacPherson's Lament* and, some months before, he had met in a pub—a haunt of folk singers —a man who had sung a song he had composed about the boxer Benny Lynch. But classical music he found dead, not to say boring. He couldn't see the point of it, or ballet or opera. But the trouble was that he respected it and did not blame it, but rather blamed himself, as if he had an organ missing. There must have been something to all these people,

Mozart and Beethoven, all these gigantic people, there must have been something to Michelangelo, da Vinci and Rubens and so on. But to him they seemed somehow statuesque, distant, composing or drawing or painting or sculpting for a different race, a larger, more solid race. They were like large boulders on a hill.

When he was young he used to read the comics and still did so now and again, though he wondered what Dixon would think of that. It occurred to him for the first time that though he himself often speculated about Dixon he had never asked himself what Dixon would think of him. Surely Dixon would disapprove of his reading the comics.

Tom liked the comics for the same reason as he liked jazz, their spontaneity, their unpredictable nature and also their bright colours, their vulgar yellows and crimsons. But he would never have told anyone that he loved reading them, that Desperate Dan was one of his heroes. When he was young, lying in bed with bronchitis, he used to read them by the hour. Sometimes, when he remembered that barrow episode, he thought that it was exactly the kind of thing that would happen to Desperate Dan, in that world where hats flew off, there were shouts of *aargh* and *oops*, and everything came right in the end. But he was often ashamed of all that and also the fact that he sometimes read picture books about the war. He felt that he ought to be reading better books, that he should be listening to classical music and that he shouldn't be dwelling too often in that irresponsible world of crazy hosepipes and flung pies and dishelmeted policemen, all falling about in a crimson sky.

For this reason he kept all his comics locked away in a drawer and his books by Hesse and other authors carefully visible. Not that anyone visited much. But in case anyone did. Though at the same time he wasn't so careful about hiding his jazz records. Jazz was respectable. There were columns about jazz in dignified newspapers, though none about comics. He thought of the jazz musicians as orphans trying to create music from the fragments of the city. He thought of them as vulnerable wanderers. Sometimes in the city where he lived he could see tricks of the light which reminded him of the precariousness and lovableness of jazz, vistas at the end of streets, unfinished glimpses.

But these visitations were not frequent. Most of the time the city was grey and dull and he only stayed in it because he could find bits of work to do there more easily than he could anywhere else. A lot of the time the city was dispiriting and desolating and ugly. Certainly not like the world of Dixon, not like the world of Mozart. The city was uncivilised.

After he had written the bit about Dixon meeting the girl he put on his record of *Finlandia* and tried to concentrate on it and decide whether Dixon would like it. He thought on the whole that perhaps it was too melancholy for Dixon, too pastoral, too northern. And yet he wasn't sure. On the other hand the *1812 Overture* almost certainly wouldn't do. He would really have to borrow some Mozart. Perhaps Ann liked Mozart and had some records or knew where he could get hold of them. Perhaps she could tell him things that he didn't know about, introduce him to a new area of experience, one which he could make use of in his writing. Though really he didn't feel that she was at all cultural. She was probably not musical at all. On the other hand, he couldn't imagine her liking pop songs, for example. And almost certainly not jazz.

For the tenth time he played the *Finlandia* while, in the house below, the untamed dog barked at his master, endlessly snapping its teeth. It was very odd that, really, he found himself thinking again. Perhaps that was how marriage was,

73

his own mother and father, for instance, the latter trying to sit quietly and his own mother barking at him. Perhaps the man and the dog formed a strange marriage. "Bugger you," he shouted down, at the same time taking off the record. "Why don't you get rid of that dog? Do you need him so much? He ought to be taken somewhere and shot." But every day the old man would plod along with the dog rearing up and snapping at him continually. How he could stand it was beyond Tom's understanding, for the dog really looked ferocious. "Ah, to hell with you," he said again and went over to the cupboard. He took out a packet of soup and began to make some. He had done one hour's writing that day, which wasn't really bad. He might get some more done before the night was over. He usually worked better at night, his mind felt clearer, and the dog didn't disturb him. There was an eeriness about the night which he loved, and he would listen to the clicking of heels on the road, eventually fading into silence. Sometimes he would go to the window and look out at the blazing moon with its stunning clarity hidden now and again by a cloud, a big infertile stone which at the same time looked romantic and free.

II

W H E N T O M A R R I V E D at the cinema Ann was there before him waiting. He saw her before she saw him, framed in the neon light, in the blue coat and hat which she had put on for the occasion. He stood watching her for a moment, reminded of a story which he had read in a newspaper about a husband and wife in their sixties who had met for the first time in a cinema and who re-enacted every year that meeting, he going to the row where he had met her and she waiting there for him. Dixon would have found this sentimental but Tom found the tale curiously moving. Dixon might have met someone outside the door of an opera house perhaps, but he couldn't imagine him rehearsing that story in real life. He couldn't imagine himself doing it either. He couldn't imagine Dixon running, filled with joy as a sail with a breeze.

As he watched her she seemed to take on solidity, to grow more definite. She wasn't particularly looking anywhere that he could see. She wasn't even glancing at her watch. She was simply waiting patiently, serenely. As people milled about her, some studying the trailer and some going straight into the cinema, he thought of her as solid and vulnerable at the same time. She wasn't aware that he was looking at her, and this made her endearing and fragile. But what filled him with a rare joy was that she was waiting for him. The world, the universe, steadied around her, took on shape and meaning. The very fact of her existence, of her waiting, was enough for that to happen. She was like a magnet which attracted filings. Abruptly, as if aware of the possibility of voyeurism in the situation, he moved forward. What a terrible thing to be looked at like that! For after all she wasn't a rose or a stone, she was a human being. It was indecent to be trapped by his gaze in that ring of neon.

He walked briskly forward and said, "Here I am." She looked at him. He wasn't wearing his khaki coat. He was wearing instead a grey suit and a collar and tie. His bright hair, though long, was brushed and he seemed very presentable. She was flattered that he had gone to the length of improving his appearance, though she didn't comment on it.

"Shall we go in?" she said. She waited for him while he went over to the booth and bought two tickets. She noticed with concern that he had bought two of the most expensive tickets, sensing that he didn't have very much money. They walked together up the wide steps, past the beribboned commissionaire, into the opulent interior with its plush seats. They sat beside each other while the music played before the film began and the lights shone with a dark red lustre. The curtains were still drawn. The room was filling up rapidly as if it were a theatre. She saw that there was a clock set in the ceiling directly ahead and that it registered six o'clock.

"Would you like some sweets?" he asked her.

"Not really," she said, arranging herself comfortably in the seat. It was a very luxurious place really but she didn't much care for the seat. Tom was sitting on her left not saying much at first. Then he began to talk about the Western and she was surprised to find how intense and interesting he was. But she felt that he was still not aware of her in a real way and that he seemed to be thinking of her in relation to another world, another context. She found this rather queer and nearly said something to him but decided against it. After all, she might not see him again after that night. She hadn't yet made up her mind about him though certainly he had gone up in her estimation by the clothes he wore. That had shown a certain care and sensitivity.

He was saying that the best Western was *Shane* followed by *High Noon*. She had never seen either of them. She didn't know anything about Westerns. Her favourite films were romantic ones. The best film she had seen in recent times was *Rebecca* with Laurence Olivier. She didn't like very advanced films where the hero and the heroine were seen in bed with each other naked and sweating. The films she really liked were ones where the hero and heroine were reconciled to each other after a certain amount of complication.

He was saying that the idea of the Western was basically that of the chase, and that was why it was suited to the cinema. The cowboy, he remarked, was always lonely, he was not an admirable person, he was not self-sufficient. People didn't seem to realise that to wander about as he did was the action of a lonely man. The purest cowboy idea was that of the cowboy playing a guitar to himself under the stars. It was the essence of beauty and loneliness. She thought that perhaps he saw himself as a cowboy.

In fact she considered that his conversation was a protective device designed to prevent him from talking to her at all seriously.

The music stopped and the film began. She watched it with fascination, the settler, the wife, the boy, the cowboy riding up to the homestead and asking for water for his horse. Now and again she would glance sideways at Tom and see that he was totally absorbed in what was happening. He didn't look at her at all and this in some curious way made her feel secure so that she was able to relax. The story unfolded itself slowly in the bright colours of the large screen. She saw that Shane was meant to be an emanation from the distant past but she was more interested in the relation of the wife to him than in anything else. She herself preferred the solid settler to Shane. There was something about Shane that made her feel uneasy, a sense of transience, an edginess, an orphan restlessness. He was in the society but not of it. She approved of his sentiments though. Violence was bad. One shouldn't wear a gun if one could help it.

She was interested too in the behaviour of the boy who seemed to be about the same age as the ones she herself taught. She wondered what would happen to him and whether he would be corrupted. She thought again how much her teaching had affected her in that she saw everything as either useful or not useful for educational purposes.

Once Tom touched her arm in excitement and said, "Watch this." It was the part of the film where the gunslinger, clad in black, had been taken to the ranch by Fletcher who was telling the homesteader, Starrett, to leave. The gunslinger was sitting at ease on his horse as if he owned the world, the hard sunlight defining him; and leaning against the fence with the same apparent casualness was Shane without a gun. For a moment the glances of the two men met, in a startled recognition that they were both of the same kind. It was a meaningful moment and she realised it.

And so the film proceeded towards its end. Starrett had been knocked out by Shane to prevent him being killed in the denouement, and Shane rode out alone to his rendezvous, the boy running after him. It was true that it was all taut and interesting, but at the same time she wasn't basically interested in *that*. Shane seemed unreal. She couldn't imagine being as good as that and yet as hard. She would have liked to have seen more about the relationship between him and the wife. Gunfighting didn't interest her. It was too easy a way out. She preferred the slow, almost sluggish, plodding Starrett to Shane. He seemed a more real character.

Then there was the fight in the saloon, Shane spinning round and firing upwards at the ambusher on the balcony after he had killed the gunslinger. The silence in the saloon. The music fading away in an elegiac manner. She looked at Tom who seemed perfectly rapt. She couldn't think exactly what he looked like, and then it came into her mind. He had exactly the same expression she had once seen on the face of a painting of the Virgin Mary. She started to laugh and he looked at her in amazement. When she told him he burst out laughing too. For the first time she felt some real contact. There was something else on, a film about the prairies, but Tom suddenly got up and said, "Come on, anything else would be rubbish after that." The film about the prairies would have been useful for a geography lesson but she decided not to say anything.

They emerged into the lights and stood for a moment outside the cinema. "Is there a restaurant?" he asked. As they walked along, it began to drizzle a little. They passed boys and girls walking arm in arm, and a group of skinheads who looked bleak and monkish in the harsh light. They passed a dance hall which was painted a bright and awful green. They passed skinny lovers embracing in closes scarred with gang names, till they eventually found a restaurant. It was a Chinese restaurant and they sat as before in a corner.

This time he wouldn't let her pay for anything and he told her this before they started. It looked quite an expensive restaurant, dimly lit, music leaking from the walls.

"What did you think of the film?" he asked. She had taken off her coat and he saw that she was wearing an attractive blue dress which matched her eyes and a large emerald brooch at her breast.

"I thought it was very good," she said. "What did you think of the wife?"

"What wife?" he said.

"Mrs Starrett, was that her name? She seemed to be in love with Shane."

"Oh, I see. Yes, I suppose she was, now that you mention it."

"I noticed it. I thought there would have been more about that."

"What did you think of Shane himself?"

"He was all right. He seemed rather strange."

"How do you mean strange?"

He seemed not really to be listening to her. She noticed that he had cut himself shaving. She still felt that they were strangers, that he was examining her, that he was watching her, studying her.

"Well, he didn't seem to belong anywhere. I wondered where he was going at the end."

"He was supposed to be a man dedicated to something," he said.

After a while she said, "It's very expensive here. Are you sure that we wouldn't be better . . ."

"No, we'll eat here. I have some money."

At that moment the waiter came up and they ordered curries. He ate quickly and she more slowly. She wondered what she was doing there at all, but if she hadn't been she would have been at home working on projects and she was tired of them.

"Tell me about your book," she said. "You said you were trying to write a book. What's it about? It's not a Western, is it?"

"Good Lord, no," he said in surprise, "it's not a Western. I'm not good enough to write a real Western. It's not a very

80

good novel. It's silly and pointless. I may never finish it."

"But surely you can if you want to," she said.

"It's not like that," he said in a sudden burst of energy. "It's not like that at all. It's not a matter of the will, like trying to learn a bicycle. It's got to be waited for. Sometimes I can't write anything. Anyway it's no good. But I want to finish it. After that I'll see."

"Why isn't it a matter of the will?" she probed, eating slowly.

"You have to wait," he said, looking at her for the first time directly as if he were really seeing her. "You have to wait. You can't go on day after day. You could decide to spend hours on it but it might not be any good. It's not a routine thing. Do you understand?"

"I think so," she said, though she didn't really. In her experience if you worked hard enough, if you decided on something, you could do anything you liked. It was all a question of determination.

"Where did you get the brooch from?" he asked suddenly.

"It was my mother's," she said.

"It's very pretty," he said as if embarrassed. "It suits you. It really does. Are you liking the food?"

"Yes," she said, "it's very nice."

The trouble was that they didn't seem to have any small talk. She felt that he was trying to talk but couldn't find anything to talk about, as if his obsessions were elsewhere.

"I . . ." They both began to speak at the same time and then stopped embarrassed.

"Tell me about your projects," he said.

"Oh, they're not terribly interesting. One is called *Dress Down the Ages*. We did a lot of work on that."

"I see."

Somehow she felt that he would find the project trivial

81

and didn't wish to talk about it. And she supposed that on one level it was, all that cutting of pictures out of newspapers and magazines, and pasting them into notebooks. To him that would appear superficial.

It wasn't really being a very successful evening.

"Can you give me your address or your phone number?" he suddenly asked.

"If you'd like it," she said. It was difficult to say no, though at the same time she wasn't all that sure she wanted to see him again. So she wrote it down for him though she said he wasn't to phone her at the school. The headmaster didn't like personal phone calls coming through on the school switchboard.

Near them two young people were sitting opposite each other gazing into each other's eyes, their hands clasped above the table. The light was gentle and unglaring and she felt at ease in the room. It reminded her of early days spent lying under leaves in green woods when she wanted to be alone. She had a sudden impulse to straighten his tie but his face looked moody and distant and she didn't think he would want her to touch him. She thought of him as unfinished and needing to be put together. But she didn't have the knowledge or expertise to set about doing it, and she sensed that if she tried to do anything like that he would withdraw again. She couldn't understand why he was interested in her. She sensed a fierce inarticulate rage deep within him as if some force in him was trying to get out.

"Are you ready?" she said at last.

They got up, he paid, and they walked out together into the light of the city which seemed to make them smaller as they emerged. Instinctively they drew closer to each other. The buildings around them were tall, there was a jigsaw of shining lights on the road. To each of them simultaneously there came a chilling haunting wind of separateness. Without thinking she put her hand on his arm and he let it rest there. She didn't know what he was thinking. The rain had stopped and they left the slummy area and came out into an area of more space. They crossed a bridge and he stopped and stared down into the water.

Their heads close to each other, he said, "Sometimes I want desperately to be alone. Do you ever need to be alone?"

With a spirit of gaiety she said, "Like Greta Garbo," and had an image of Greta Garbo in a long coat walking up an avenue with autumn leaves all round her and a dying music following her.

"Yes," he shouted gaily, "like Greta Garbo. I vant to be alone." He faced the city and shouted in a German voice, "I vant to be alone. I do not vant ze Common Market." She was amazed at this sudden transformation, this ebullience. "Bring me my bow of burning gold," he shouted, "and also, if you have ze time, my arrows of desire. Also pick up my chariot." He looked suddenly gay and clownish in the harlequin lights.

Suddenly he started whirling round and round in a gay invented dance and then came back to her and took her by the arm. "You Tarzan, me Shane," he said and burst out laughing. Then she burst out laughing as well. They walked briskly together down the long road till they came to her bus stop. She waved at him out of the bus wondering if she would see him again but sensing deep down that she would. He waved back furiously and then turned away. She watched him from the window of the stationary bus. He looked suddenly part of what her life had become. He was a recognisable person among the streets and the stones, in a city being torn down and rebuilt.

12

*Dixon and Sheila stood in the foyer of the concert hall,
Dixon dressed in white shirt and cravat and carrying a cane,
Sheila dressed in a long trailing blue gown which, Dixon
thought, didn't suit her. Perhaps she hadn't been going to
concerts in the past, perhaps she didn't like music. And yet
music was very important to Dixon, especially the music of
Mozart. He whistled a Mozart tune while he waited to go
in, hoping that he wouldn't meet anyone he knew, which in
fact was extremely unlikely since he didn't often go to this
particular place. He noticed that Sheila was gazing at the
dresses the other women were wearing with a certain envy.
She seemed ill at ease; was it because she was with him? He
couldn't tell. She was carrying a large blue handbag which
seemed unsuitable. He would have to get her new clothes, he
would have to dress her.*

*With a practised mind he absorbed the scene around him.
Always there was that small crystal which was ticking over
in his mind and which made him see everything in terms of
the novel. He glanced at the three women sitting at the low
table and tabulated them as unmarried lecturers talking in
their usual brittle, intellectual manner. He studied the men
in tails and dinner shirts standing at the bar, looking over
each other's shoulders. He watched the commissionaire who
stood at the door proprietorially in his military ribbons.*

"Would you like a drink?" he asked her.

"No," she said, "not really."

"Well, in that case hadn't we better go in?"

They went in and found their seats. It wasn't a very large place but it looked luxurious with its clock set in the ceiling and its plushy seats.

"Have you listened to much music before?" he asked her, unfolding the programme he had bought.

"No, I haven't." He glanced sideways at her. She still seemed uneasy, in a strange place. He smiled inwardly. Certainly his former wife would never have come at all; she thought music was ridiculous and was bored easily. He didn't think this girl would show boredom. Perhaps she was used to boredom in her orphan world. He thought of the book he was working on, in which he had torn to pieces the woman he had left, transforming her into the brittle spirit of a world dominated by barbarians. There he took his revenge on her, calmly and slowly and with immense leisured satisfaction. In order to do it, he had to leave her. He had to hate her sufficiently and that wasn't difficult, she had hurt him enough. The first pages were going all right but he did find the day long without her. There was a certain hectic combative excitement that he missed.

There was some applause as the orchestra took their seats. The first item on the programme was the 1812 Overture. It wasn't one of his favourite pieces of music. Still, it might appeal to Sheila. He listened without much interest, though there was no doubt that Tchaikovsky had a certain naive tunefulness. But he wasn't a great composer. These long languorous stretches alternating with bouts of violent action. Descriptive music of this nature was a denial of true music, its essential quality.

He handed Sheila the programme and she studied it. He liked looking at her sideways, noticing her clear pure profile, her quiet competent appearance. She didn't speak much because this wasn't a situation that she felt at home in. He

85

liked that. He liked the fact that she wouldn't speak when she had nothing to say. Her bowed neck and head looked vulnerable and helpless.

The Overture accelerated to a frenzied clash of arms, cavalry, horses, swish of sabres. No, this wasn't really his music. It was too active, not intellectual enough, lacking in true feeling, superficial. Sheila unearthed some sweets and gave him one. He gazed at them bemusedly and then tasted the mint on his tongue. He watched a musician staring at his score in a bored manner, not at that point playing. Napoleon. Ah, there was a hero, the man with the broken star wandering dazedly through the snow which destroyed him. What thoughts he must have had, how he must have suffered. Josephine, palaces, men eating each other at fires on that terrible march, the star fading behind the snow, the ghostly riders hemming them in, the squat little emperor with his contempt for the proles. Ah, there was a man. There was a mind. If only one could put him down on paper, if only one could make him credible.

The music ended. Grand old Russia had ejected the germ that troubled her sleep. He thought of shadow after shadow crossing the snow towards France, never to arrive there.

Sheila was sitting beside him, composed and calm. Perhaps he could rely on her, relax after the storm. But then how could one know?

He looked at the programme. Sibelius. Not particularly good either. Still, he was melancholy and smooth. A landscape of water. He laughed at the paradox. The music unfolded in his mind, distant and cold and melancholy. He wanted to say something to Sheila but he couldn't think of anything to say. She too looked distant in her blue gown. Perhaps she had borrowed it, perhaps it wasn't her own.

Melancholy music, a composer far from the centre of

things, buried in a dream of a country that he had remade in his imagination. Romanticism. Perhaps, unlike Sibelius, that was what he should do; go out into the streets, confront and assume the brutalities, as some of the reviewers had told him to do. But, ah, think of Mozart. Did he do that? Surely not. That sublime gift had nothing to do with any age, it was as natural as breathing.

At the interval they stood in the foyer again.

"How did you like it?" he asked her.

"It was beautiful," she said but he sensed that she really hadn't been impressed. Music was perhaps not one of her things, not one of her interests. He didn't know what her interests were. He asked her.

"I do a lot of embroidery," she said. "And I paint in an amateurish way."

He shuddered. Of course she would paint in an amateurish way. Yet perhaps embroidery suited her. It accounted for her air of calm. He wondered about her for a moment, about her background, who her mother had been, and her father, about her impressionable years.

"Most of us do things in an amateurish way," he said at last. He didn't believe that he himself was an amateur but he thought this was the thing to say.

"Do you want to go back for the rest of the concert then?" he asked. She waited for him to make up his mind. True, he thought, there was Mozart and he would like to hear him.

"If you aren't enjoying it," he said, "we'll go for a meal."

"But I am," she said.

"No," he said making a decision, "we'll definitely go for a meal. We'll catch up on some music some other time." They went out into the street which was all yellow and red. In front of the concert hall was a building painted a livid green from which deafening sounds of music blasted. It sounded as if a hundred sets of guitars and drums were hammering away simultaneously. He felt her interest quicken but they walked on across a bridge that banged in the wind. He often wished that he could drive and thanked God that it wasn't raining.

They entered a hotel and went straight to the dining room. They ordered. He wondered about his feelings for her. He thought her nice and relaxing and he felt peaceful with her. He had really wanted to get away from that set, his wife and her friends. He wanted away from their abrasiveness. But was that a weakness in him? If he was a good novelist ought he not to be more ruthless, ought he not have fought them on their own ground? Had he run away? And what was his writing anyway? Was it an activity that did not belong to the real world? But still these people wouldn't give him any peace. Their tongues clacked bitterly all day. And he needed peace, he needed space and time for things to grow in him, to come to birth. They wouldn't allow him his quiet pregnancies. Perhaps she might.

Of course there was no guarantee that she would have anything to do with him.

"Have you ever thought of getting married?" he said casually, watching the waiter come up with some wine.

"I've never been asked," she said clearly and almost humorously.

He laughed. "Oh, I don't believe that." They drank their soup quickly for it was a cold night. He would have to get a taxi for her when they left.

"It's true," she said. "Other girls seem to get married easily but not me." He wondered about that: perhaps there was something wrong with her. And yet there didn't seem to be.

"I think," he said carefully, pouring her out some wine,

"there's something you should know. I'm parted from my wife."

"Thank you for telling me."

She asked no questions. Was this because she had guessed already, or was it because she was indifferent, or was it because she didn't know what to say? What did she think of him? Did she regard him as the suave, confident man of the world?

"Could I see one of your books some time?" she asked him.

"Certainly. I can give you copies of most of them. I would sign them for you if you would like that."

"If you would," she said.

They ate their fish.

She looked around her and said, "I don't think I should like to live in a hotel. It would be very lonely."

"I'm sure it would," he said. In fact that was why he hadn't come to live in a hotel himself. It was too formal, too chilly. He preferred being where he was, at least for the time being.

"Would you like to go to an opera next week?" he asked. "Or would you like to visit me? I could play you some of my gramophone records. Would you like that?"

After some hesitation she said that she would.

He gave her the address and she copied it down into a small book that she took out of her purse.

"I stay with a girl friend, so I'm afraid I can't invite you," she said. Sometimes he caught her gazing past him with a distant gaze; it was at such moments that he sensed what her life had been like. And yet she seemed warm and pleasant and companionable and he felt relaxed in her company, though he missed perhaps some of the wit and malice and sardonic chatter of his first wife. Or did he really

89

miss it? Perhaps it was just that he wasn't as yet used to these human silences.

There was hardly anyone in the dining room except themselves and they finished their meal in silence. He felt that she was still wary of him, as if she didn't know what to say.

As she said that she wanted to be home early he went to the phone and ordered a taxi for her. They drank their coffee till the taxi came. He felt a happy calm companionship. There was about her the air of one who throws herself on the world, undisguised. She had a girlish appearance, a sincerity, which appealed to him more than ever after his experiences. He couldn't afford to lose her.

He put her in the taxi and watched it drive away. Then he began walking, as the night wasn't wet though it was slightly chilly. He began composing in his mind certain sentences connected with his book but found that they didn't come with any urgency. There was no fire about them, no headlong fierce arrival. He worried this through as he made his way along the fiery streets, thinking of the flat awaiting him, with its books and records and radio. He would have to get some work done. After all, there was the world of the lucid intelligences of his novel to strengthen, to make plausible and realistic, rather as in the work of Hesse, though he wouldn't admit to anyone that he had read the German author from whom he had borrowed so many of his ideas, who had taught him to write with a cool metaphysical poise, such as was possible in the eighteenth century. The bridge banged noisily about him in the wind as he walked along it, lights shining all round him. A large stout drunken woman with a red face waddled along, talking to herself restlessly. She made strange signals to him but he ignored them. She *was too red and raw and typical to fit into any of his books: anyway he didn't know what language she would speak. Against the parapet of the bridge a girl and a boy embraced fiercely, the boy almost forcing her over into the river as he bent her backwards like a bow, descending on her with hungry beak and body.*

13

ANN CAME INTO the room with a tray on which there were small biscuits with toasted cheese. She was wearing a red dress with yellow flowers on it. She seemed calm and poised among the noise and swirl that was going on in the flat. Sitting on the floor or on sofas were about eight people whom Tom had never met till that night. Ann stopped to talk to a tall thin fellow with a wispy yellowish beard. Tom watched her. Ann had told him that now and again she and her flatmate Mary held a party to which there came mostly Mary's friends as she wasn't long out of college. On a chair a tall youth with a pelt of hair was singing to himself a folk song in a sonorous sad voice while at his feet a girl in a kilt sat looking up at him soulfully.

Tom drank another whisky and stared angrily at the wallpaper which was red on one wall and black on the opposite. He felt out of things and couldn't understand why he had come, especially as Ann was talking to that thin idiot about education and he hadn't seen much of her during the course of the night. Now and again he could hear phrases about requisitions and books and classes. The tall thin idiot was holding a glass of sherry in his hand and Ann was looking up at him, pretty and vivacious in her red dress. He opened a can of lager which he found beside him on the floor and drank thirstily.

A large placid fellow beside him said that he taught physics. What did Tom teach?

"I don't teach," said Tom curtly. "I don't teach anybody anything."

Mop-hair had stopped singing and was leaning down to kiss the girl whose arm rested on his knee. Tom's eye was drawn to the cream-coloured clock on the mantelpiece which showed half past one. He was mesmerised by it and in his state of drunkenness was trying to make out whether he could see the hand moving. Time, what was it? How was it created? He felt suddenly terribly sad, and weighed down by a premonition of some disaster sailing towards him, a black ship which neither *bons mots* nor wit could divert and which was present for everybody at the best of times.

A small man with a beard appeared suddenly at his side. "Ann tells me that you are a writer," he said. His wet eyes looked melancholy and spiteful.

"I haven't written anything," said Tom to whom his voice suddenly seemed very loud. "I try."

"I write a bit," said the small man, offering his hand. "My name's Eddy. I write poetry. Of course I don't have much time. The curse of writers."

"What do you do?" asked Tom without much interest.

"I work in an office. You don't know Lorimer, do you? He's a nice writer. Writes poems, and paints. Or Mason? You don't know any of them?"

"No," said Tom, "I don't know any of them." His mouth seemed to be full of pebbles and fog and the girl's kilt swayed redly in front of him.

"Well," said Eddy, "I thought I'd ask. I hope you don't mind my asking. I write concrete poems you know. Like Lorimer. We are thinking of bringing out a pamphlet."

"Are you?" said Tom. What the hell was Ann finding to talk about?

Yes. We can flog it round the pubs. Of course the

established names hog everything. You can't get into the poetry anthologies. Have you ever tried to get in?"

"No," said Tom.

Eddy took out a grubby piece of paper from some deep recess in his jacket and said, "Would you care to give an opinion of this?" At first Tom thought he was going to bring out a pound note which he would have much appreciated. He stared distastefully down at the paper which looked black and soiled.

It said:

> Dawn
> rises
> like a fart over the Clyde

Tom put it down on the small table in front of him and sighed heavily. The little man picked the paper up angrily and stalked away. Later Tom could see him talking to the two who were embracing on the floor and laughing. He felt very very aggressive and frustrated and rather drunk.

He heard someone beside him say, "Of course education is different nowadays. We have to make it relevant. We have to show them the point of what we're doing." He saw that it was the thin man who had been talking to Ann. He turned away and drank another whisky. He felt as if he wanted to smash the whole room and uproot the chairs. A wave of mediocrity hit him like a stench. He himself felt mediocre and unreal, as if he were drifting about like a fog. In front of him in a corner he saw a pile of records, some Mozart, and some Edith Piaf and some Scottish folk songs. His eyes moved slowly up to where he saw a picture of a deer standing above a swirling river with a green mountain in the background. He suddenly wanted to be there, wherever it was, away from these people and away from Dixon, somewhere clean and pure and uncorrupted. He wondered what Ann was playing at, bringing him here and talking to that thin drip.

A large man eased himself across the floor and put a record on the record player. Suddenly everybody was standing up and dancing, moving their bodies sensuously and rhythmically, clicking their fingers, dreaming a dream, all except himself and the long drip and Ann. The dancers looked like stems with flowers on their tops, self-obsessed, lost in themselves, pre-Raphaelite people. He felt very lonely and suddenly piercingly aware of the premonition he had sensed before. He poured himself another beer and drank it. The drip was staring sardonically at the dancers and saying, "Relevance is of course the secret. Have you ever seen *Top of the Pops*? That's exactly how they look. That's what our pupils imitate. That's what they know about. All they know about."

Tom felt the rage rising in him like bile. He would have to leave before he did something outrageous. Ann was now beside him. She said, "Are you enjoying yourself?"

He didn't trust himself to say anything but perhaps she saw some terrible hostility in his eyes, for she added quickly, "Have you got enough to drink?" He saw her as a stranger, as belonging to the hostile world. He studied her coldly and distantly. There were wrinkles under her eyes and she looked tired. Perhaps she didn't like these parties after all.

"Would you like to sit down here," he said, "beside me?"

"I have to get more food," she said. He felt her also withdrawing into her orphan world.

"Can't your flatmate do that?" he asked angrily. The tall drip was looking down at him from about fifteen feet. He wanted to kick him in the teeth, to cram all his mediocrity

95

down his throat. He felt a storm raging inside his head, the crackle of electricity.

"She needs help," said Ann, "she's been working hard all night."

"Christ," he said through his teeth.

The tall drip said to him, "Have you ever seen *Top of the Pops*?"

"Oh, shut your stupid mouth," said Tom and turned abruptly away. The dancers were swaying backwards and forwards, some more fluid and relaxed than others. A huge man, vast as a boulder, thrust out a huge behind. Tom's eyes rested on the picture again. Ah, to be in that place of deer and shepherds and no guitars.

Ann was just passing with a tray. He said, "I'm leaving."

She laid the tray down on a table and came to the door with him, sensing his anger.

"What's wrong?" she asked.

"I've been here all night," he said, "and you've hardly spoken a word to me."

"I thought you'd like to . . ." she started. In her eyes there was an unholy joy and they sparkled beautifully.

"I'm bloody well going home," he said. "I can't stand your bloody stupid friends." His hand rested on the knob of the door.

"If that's what you think—" she said, "if that's your opinion . . ."

"That's what I think," he said.

"All right then," she said.

"All right then," he said.

"They're nice people. They're Mary's friends, not mine. I don't see why you can't talk to them."

"They're bloody bores," he said. "That's what they are,

bloody bores. Thanks for the whisky." He was almost crying with frustration and rage.

"Goodbye," he said.

"Goodbye," she said.

He slammed the door behind him and ran down the stairs into the air. He felt light-headed. And yet he was daunted by what he had done. At least the party would give him some copy for his book, but what would happen to Dixon now that there was no Ann for him to be with? What would happen to his own book? But he was so blinded with rage that he didn't care. He cursed monotonously under his breath as he strode on, feeling the satisfaction of having burned his boats, feeling the anger on his tongue, inside his stomach like whisky. Bugger the lot of you, he kept repeating. And especially you, he said to the Ann in his mind, seeing her in her red dress with the wrinkles under her eyes. He felt that he must keep his pride somehow. He wasn't going to a place where he didn't know anyone and be treated like that. He wasn't a serf, was he?

As he walked under the million stars he calmed down and became more philosophical, more like Dixon. He thought, This must have been what Dixon felt when he walked out on that bitchy wife of his. Dixon would have to find someone else or he himself would project Ann, the unwon Ann, into the rest of the novel. He wasn't going to be made a fool of. Not even for Dixon would he do that. Not for anyone.

He imagined he heard a voice calling him and looked back along the long street but there was no one there. He could hear only the echo of his own feet. Now he was more calm and not at all angry. He could see things very clearly, the haloes round the lamp posts, their brooding professorial stance. In the distance he heard a train screaming through the night. A line came into his mind, "Somewhere beyond

97

the stars with you." It was from an old song that he had heard on TV recently. Bugger her, that was the last he would see of her, that was for sure. He'd had enough. She wasn't going to make a fool of him. No one was.

In the light ahead of him he saw a man seated on the pavement reading a book. The book was red and looked as if it was burning. The man was in rags sitting there as if beside a brazier. He too looked red. It couldn't be true, of course. It must be a nightmare. And sure enough when he arrived at the spot there was no one there, there was nothing there. He passed his hand across his brow, frightened, and walked over. He knelt by the side of the road and tried to be sick. All the time he thought he was hearing a voice calling him back, but there was no voice, only the vast glittering night.

It was after two in the morning and he wanted to go to bed. He felt frantically in his pocket to make sure that he hadn't lost his key. But it was there all right. He put it back and hurried on. But he kept his fingers round it, frightened that even yet he might lose it. He staggered onwards singing to himself to keep his courage up and now and again breaking off and swearing.

14

THE FOLLOWING DAY he stayed in bed late. He felt rotten. He didn't want to go out and he didn't want to eat. When he did get up he wandered restlessly from chair to window, now and again picking up a book and dropping it. He didn't know what was wrong with him. A dull rage burned in him steadily and he felt as if he had been betrayed. He thought he'd do some work on his book but he couldn't bring himself to touch it. Later on, perhaps. He knew now that he would have to find another Ann. This new Ann would not act as the one in real life had done. She would have to be much more composed and warm, less distant. To hell with her, he thought.

He sat in the chair and listened to someone pacing overhead. This was another man who lived alone and didn't sleep much but sometimes brought friends to his flat who stayed up late and drank and sang. He didn't even know what job the man did or whether he had a job. At nights he could hear him go downstairs, presumably to walk the streets endlessly, as his insomniac mind could no longer bear the closeness of his room.

There was nothing on TV worth watching. There was just the usual comic rubbish which made the mind blank after a while. Sometimes he thought of throwing the set away and going back to radio, but he didn't. He was always hoping that one day or night an experience of true purity would emerge from the shadowy rubbish on the screen, that it would appear like a true great picture, calm and pure and glowing and immediate, such that for ever afterwards he would remember it. The only thing of that quality he had seen was *Citizen Kane* but that had only been one experience in years.

In the course of the soggy afternoon the doorbell rang and he ran to it, half hoping that it might be Ann, but it wasn't. The stair was dark, and the day rainy and wet, and the window on the stair dim and dusty. Standing at the door were a man and a girl both encased in plastic raincoats. He wondered at first whether he ought to know them but it turned out that they were Jehovah's Witnesses.

The girl whose plastic coat streamed with rain, said :

"We are from the Jehovah's Witnesses. Are you interested in religion? Are you at all interested in religion?" Her dull zealous eyes examined him. The tall thin youth stared at him. There was a carbuncle on his face.

"I'm sorry, I . . ." He was about to shut the door. The woman said, "What do you think about peace? Do you think man will ever find a way to peace?"

"I don't know," he said, "I don't really . . ." He still burned with rage but he couldn't bring himself to shut the door in their faces. Dixon would never get involved in situations like this, ridiculous pseudo-religious dialogues on a dusty dark stair.

"Have you ever thought about the Meaning of Life?" she said. He almost burst out laughing. What a ludicrous question! Who did these people think they were? Did they have a monopoly on the Key to the Universe in Six Easy Lessons? What did they think he was, some silly moron who had never read a book, who never thought about anything beyond food and drink? In what closed world did they live? Imagine being so humourless as to ask such a question! He noticed that the light from the stair window was getting dimmer and switched the electric light on. In the harsh light he saw the rain dripping steadily from their yellow plastic coats. The two faces sprang suddenly into focus.

Suddenly for the first time the youth spoke. He had a stutter. He spoke quickly and nervously, "Don't you think that the Lord's disciples showed us how to live in peace?"

"I thought they quarrelled among themselves," said Tom contemptuously. The girl looked at him in surprise as if some warning signal had been received by her dim mind.

But the tall youth continued, "But Christ was God. He was the Son of God."

"Lots of people think they are God," said Tom as cuttingly as he could. "People in asylums think they're God. They also think they are made of glass." He nearly said, "They may even think they are Jehovah's Witnesses." What an absurd situation. What would Dixon think of it? Would he have quoted Voltaire at them?

The youth smiled in a sickly manner and the girl smiled too but more warily. Tom suddenly thought, I wonder if I can use this in a novel, and was immediately interested. At that moment he didn't see them as they were, but rather as characters, as types. He wondered. Do they have a car? Do they travel about? Are they trained?

"You seem an intelligent man," said the girl. "Do you think man is capable of solving his problems alone?"

"I don't know and I don't care," said Tom. "I don't know and I couldn't care less."

"But what about the starving people of the world?" stuttered the youth. "What about pollution?"

"I don't know anything about them," said Tom. "More wars have been caused by religion than by anything else. That is one thing I know."

The girl, who looked pale in the bleak light, said in a more companionable tone, "What do you do yourself then?" She seemed puzzled by him, by his bearing and behaviour.

At this point he didn't know what to say. He had been about to say, "I am a writer," but he couldn't bring himself to do so. The claim suddenly sounded presumptuous. He wondered if Dixon would have said it, and thought that perhaps he would. Dixon would have the right hauteur. Dixon would have the correct contempt for this charade.

"I don't do anything," he said at last.

They looked at him almost in surprise.

Then the man said, "We call round at intervals. We could discuss this with you, if you like. Man cannot live on his own without anyone. We could talk to you and your wife."

"I haven't got a wife," said Tom and again felt a certain emptiness. Why was he confessing his affairs to these people? It occurred to him that it was odd not to have a wife.

The youth, who had a prominent Adam's apple, was saying, "Man cannot live except by each word that proceeds out of the mouth of God."

Tom thought, I don't have a wife, and I live alone. Have these people been sent to judge me on this dull afternoon? Why were they interrogating him anyway? What right did they have to ring his bell and ask him these silly questions? Invading his privacy.

He heard himself shouting, "I don't know what you're talking about." For some reason he associated them with the *Reader's Digest*.

"I see," said the tall youth down whose coat the rain was streaming on to the landing, on to the scruffy rug.

The girl said, as if he hadn't spoken, "Man cannot live by bread alone. That's what it says in the Bible. The disciples died happily. We know that. That's evidence, isn't it?"

"No, it's not. It's not evidence of anything. We don't know

that they died happily. Buddhists have died happily in Vietnam. They burned themselves. That doesn't prove anything."

What was he doing talking to them anyway? What would Kafka have said to them? He despised their minds so much. He didn't understand what they were doing there, what he was doing there.

And yet he felt guilty. They looked so wet, encased in their transparent plastic coats. Perhaps he ought to invite them in. The thought surprised him, because it had never occurred to him before, though in fact there had been gipsies and tinkers at the door in the past, especially one bedraggled woman with two children who was looking for shoes. He hadn't given her anything.

He said, "Would you like to come in for a minute?"

"No, thank you. It's all right. Thank you all the same," said the girl. "We have a few houses to do yet."

"Thank you," said the stuttering youth. "We have here a magazine. You may have heard of it. It's called the *Watchtower.*"

He stretched out his hand for it and she said, "It costs five pence." He gave her the money and took the magazine.

They seemed to be finished with him and he watched them walk downstairs into the rainy afternoon. He took the magazine into his room and glanced at it. It had articles with headings like "Christian Tinker tells about her Conversion". He glanced briefly at the magazine and threw it into the waste paper basket.

He felt terribly restless and didn't know what to do. He couldn't settle down to write. The day had been wasted. He felt that he was struggling inside a big black cloud that was overwhelming him. Above him the man paced steadily. The bulb in his ceiling vibrated.

No, he must write. He must try to write, whatever

happened. He must get this out of his system, whatever it was. He must continue, that was all there was to do. Anyway he couldn't go out, it was too wet. It was dull and muggy, sapping his energy. He must try and create something. He must continue with what happened to Dixon when he met Sheila again. He began to write and as he did so the dim world changed again and became a concentrated small intense glow. He knew the writing was not very good but perhaps if he worked at it later, if he polished it, he might make something of it. The thing to do was to carry on anyway. That was all there was to do.

15

The fact is, thought Dixon, I've neglected the flat a bit, and as he thought this he also recalled Yeats's dictum about the perfection of the art or of the life. Now and again he would go out and buy flowers and put them in vases on the piano or on the table. Yellow was his favourite colour. He liked nothing better than to open the window in the morning and let the air into the house. He felt like a schoolboy when he entered the flat first. He luxuriated in the idea of total freedom. There was no one he would have to talk to; his mind could blossom in secrecy without interruption. He wouldn't be caught in minefields of silly quarrels which blew out of nowhere and illuminated him in an explosive silly light. But that was at the beginning. As time passed he felt a central emptiness and he even missed those same quarrels, those untidinesses, those ragged short-tempered bursts. For all around him was a perfect silence which was more than mortal could bear.

Still there was no denying that it was a comfortable flat and he could work all day if he wanted to. The people he met on the stair now and again belonged to a good class. They carried umbrellas and wore bowler hats. They looked sleek and prosperous. They nodded politely, but they looked as if they were in a hurry to get to somewhere where they had important work to do. As for himself, he was running into difficulties with his book. Some of the easy flow of his imagination seemed to have gone. He wasn't satisfied with the inhabitants of his fictional Cultured City, they seemed to have become rather priggish, and he found it difficult to visualise them clearly or to take them seriously. Their concerns lacked urgency and realism. Was that because his own concerns lacked urgency? Was it simply because he had moved into a new place? Surely it couldn't be as simple as that?

His life, until the time he had moved into the flat, had been in some ways enclosed, in others stormy. It was true that his wife had been silly and quarrelsome but at the same time she had contributed a necessary abrasiveness to his life. She had put the life into his chiselled sentences. Without her they would have been marmoreal. On the other hand, things had become more and more unendurable. She had expected him to take her out more and more and he couldn't be bothered. She had taken to giving parties to which she had invited young sarcastic people who took nothing seriously, least of all art. They lived from hand to mouth, from moment to moment, they weren't at all creative but they lived off creative people. She had cultivated a sadistic streak as if she had begun to hate and wished to destroy him.

At one time she herself had played the piano but had given it up. She never read anything but the books of fifth-rate writers who also happened to be best sellers. His life had been lived on a razor's edge. He could feel her brooding like a thunderstorm at the edge of his life, he could feel her contempt. But now she wasn't around him: there was space everywhere but the space had lost its mortal pathos, its flickers and storms of opposition. He had to fill the space with shapes and he found he couldn't do it. He wasn't sleeping very well. More and more he needed someone who could give him peace. But at the back of his mind there was a lonely un-sleeping crystal which ticked out the message that everything must be perfect, that he was a member of an elite.

He had plenty of money; there was no problem there. The problem was how to keep writing and maintain that world which was his alone and the reason for his being. Sometimes he wondered whether the growing untidiness of his house was symbolic of something but he shied away from the thought.

One day Sheila came to see him. She rang the doorbell and he opened the door. She was wearing a fur coat and red shoes. He thought of her suddenly as Little Red Riding Hood come through the forest of the city to his door. She had brought a box of biscuits.

She sat down shyly looking around her. The lounge, he realised, wasn't too bad. There were glass cases full of books carefully arranged and there was a vase with daffodils on the table.

"I shall make you some coffee," he said excitedly.

"If you like, I'll make it," she said and he allowed her to. He found pleasure in watching her as she moved about the kitchen. There were some unwashed dishes in the sink and she washed these while he sat in a chair. Her motions, he noticed, were calm and precise.

They took their coffee into the lounge and sat down and he talked. She seemed shy and self-conscious when she wasn't doing anything.

"Did you have a busy week?" he asked.

She said there had been an inspector and that he had gone over everything she had done. He had been full of airy suggestions. Good God, he thought, what a terrible life. His own memories of school were of being taught Greek and Latin by a fanatical slim man with a moustache, who had no doubt whatsoever that the Greeks and Romans had represented the real values of civilisation and that everything since then had been a drastic decline into barbarism. He didn't think she would know any Latin or Greek.

She seemed frail and precious as he looked at her, and yet also part of the real world which he knew so little about, especially in recent years. She was out in the dust and the conflict.

He offered her one of his books which was called The Changeless Crystal *and she glanced at the first page or two. This was the one about the monk who had left the monastery and gone on a journey through the forests. He couldn't make out what she thought of the blurb. He had an idea that she didn't read many books. After a while he didn't know what to say to her. Should they go out for a walk? He wondered what it meant to her to be an orphan, to have no one at all in her world. He had had someone whom he didn't like. But to be totally alone must be a real bereavement.*

There were long silences. He thought sometimes that she was rather awed by him and that she wasn't sure whether she ought to talk about her own concerns in case he found the topic trivial. But in actual fact he did want her to talk about herself. He was starved for the minutiae of existence. He encouraged her to talk about some of the people she met. He felt as if he were becoming exhausted by the flat, its vases and flowers and pots and pans. As he sat there he suddenly thought that he missed the abrasiveness of life mediated through his wife. He felt inferior to her in a way.

He took out a chess set and began to show her how to play. That first afternoon he spent naming the pieces for her. He didn't like playing chess against people. He much preferred to solve academic problems, especially two movers, at which he was quite adept. Chess he found restful but rather dry and therefore he didn't play it much. They sat for an hour while he taught her. "Next time," he said, "we'll play a game." He thought that he was a teacher too and wondered how she had assessed him in that capacity. He was patient with her though he wasn't usually very patient. And as they played they talked.

She told him about her flatmate who had various boy friends and how she had been engaged three or four times but had broken off each engagement. She said that her flatmate insisted on giving parties on which she spent a lot of money. She was very beautiful and had many friends.

"I don't suppose she's any more beautiful than you are," he said, trying to put conviction into his voice but failing, since he didn't really believe that she was beautiful. She was pretty and calm and nice, but she wasn't beautiful. Or rather her beauty was of a different order from that which he presumed her flatmate had.

At one point she arranged the flowers in the vase for him while he stood beside her in the breeze, which blew through the window and played with her hair. She looked suddenly transient and he was pierced by a strange pang such as he hadn't felt for many years.

"Tell me about your parents," he said.

"My father was a school teacher," she said. "He taught history and he was a good teacher and a perfectionist. He would spend night after night correcting piles of exercise books. He believed implicitly in the value of what he was doing."

Her mother wasn't at all like that. She despised her mother, who thought that with his ability her father should have gone further and was inclined to ridicule him. She, that is her mother, was a philistine and never read a book. Her father had been a very handsome man, distinguished looking, with a high forehead and a pale face. He looked very scholarly and walked with a slight stoop. When he died her mother went to pieces, realising that she had depended on him more than she had thought. That was really very odd. During his lifetime she had appeared the stronger of the two, finding it easy to make decisions. But then she had utterly collapsed.

She stopped talking for a moment and then said: "What are you writing just now?"

He told her a little about the book as far as he had gone, though he didn't like to do so. She listened attentively but didn't ask any questions. When he had finished she went through and washed the coffee cups. She straightened one of the pictures.

He couldn't quite analyse his own feelings. To be involved again or not? She seemed very restful, but perhaps he needed more than that. Perhaps he needed a storm of some kind to keep him working. Already as he was talking to her he was thinking about her place in the Cultured City.

His mind suddenly became cold and clear and he could see where this was going quite easily and he didn't seem to need her. As if sensing this she got up. He said that he would see her again. Where did she want to go? The zoo might be a good place; he liked looking at animals, did she? She said that she was very fond of animals; she didn't mention that she had already been at the zoo a few times with her class. He was grateful to her for coming. It was with a certain sadness however that he watched her go downstairs to enter her own world again. There was one thing sure, he wouldn't get in touch with his wife again: if she wanted to see him she would have to take the initiative. He had his own world now, with his books and pictures and this girl. He had been pleased that she had liked his Vermeer, the one with the girl pouring milk into a milk jug. It was a solid happy picture, which he loved. She would learn from him and he would learn from her. Perhaps such a life would be enough. Unless, of course, he thought with a sudden panic, she had someone else whom she was interested in. Perhaps someone else had already found her or would find her. He imagined such a person as a dark missile speeding towards her at that very moment. That would be dreadful. That would be un-imaginably dreadful.

16

A F T E R T O M H A D gone Ann ran after him, but he
had walked away so quickly and angrily that she couldn't
find him. She had returned to the house dispiritedly. Why
had she acted like that, practically ignoring him? Was it that
she had wanted to make him jealous? She was ashamed of
herself and yet angry too. He hadn't needed to be so sensitive.
She told Mary about it, but Mary had simply said, "Oh, that
fellow glowering all night in a corner. Who is he anyway?
You should tell him to go to hell."

Sometimes Ann wondered who Mary would marry. She
was a bit alabaster-like and cold and variable. At the moment
she was going with an arty bloke who talked with an affected
drawl and wore a lot of hair on his face and head. Ann knew
that she herself wanted to marry. She wasn't the type to live
forever on her own. But on the other hand Tom was a bit
odd to say the least. He flared into anger very easily and as
far as she could see he didn't have a proper job. The conservative part of her nature was a bit wary of him, and yet
there was another part which was attracted to the mysterious
smouldering quality in him.

"Do you really think I should see him again?" she asked
Mary who was combing her hair.

"Up to you. He looked a bit of a drip to me. And there
was a patch on his jacket," said Mary casually peering into
the mirror and screwing up her face. She said this quite
without emphasis as if her judgment were reasonable and
acceptable. Ann stood in the middle of the room and watched

her. Mary was very proud of her hair. She spent a lot of time on it. And it was very crisp and boyish and glistening, resting on her head like a Greek helmet. It made her look like an antique Greek such as Ann had once seen in a *Life* magazine when she was doing a project.

It was one of those moments which seem to hold the highest significance, like a vase full of sparkling water which one bears about carefully. Ann almost shook as she made the discovery. And the discovery was that the patch in the jacket had made Tom seem real for the first time. She stared at Mary astonished that she hadn't realised what she had said but Mary continued to comb her hair.

Imagine, thought Ann, making a statement like that so casually. For that matter she herself hadn't noticed the patch on the jacket. A well surged up within her full of spring water and she felt renewed and at the same time she felt pity for Mary.

To have a patch on one's jacket was a distinguishing mark. It was what separated Tom from herself, from Mary. It was what made him real.

"Yes," she said in astonishment, "he had, hadn't he?"

"We should never have asked him," said Mary, "if he can't speak to people. He pretends he's high and mighty. I know the type."

"With a patch on his jacket," said Ann for the first time speaking to Mary without awe of her superior beauty and sophistication. Mary seemed to sense this and she looked at her in surprise and said, "What's wrong with you anyway?"

"Nothing," said Ann. She wanted to burst out laughing. Her hero with a patch on his jacket.

But at the same time she knew that it wasn't going to be easy.

"I think I shall go and see him," she said.

"You must be off your nut," said Mary.

"How can I tell what he's like till I go and see him?" said Ann. But she did know what he was like. He was different from Mary's arty friends. He wasn't affected.

"It's your life," said Mary, dismissing her and turning away into her dream. There was one thing about Mary's friends, none of them had a patch on his jacket. None of them needed to have their jackets mended. And she felt that there was some odd significance in that.

"What have you done with the needle and thread?" she asked Mary.

"I've no idea," said Mary.

Ann searched and found them inside a green box. She put both in her handbag and said, "Be seeing you." She ran down into the street which seemed suddenly alive and full of interesting people. She patted the head of a boy who was kicking a rainbow-coloured football against a railing. After she had passed him she looked back but in fact there was no patch on his sleeve or his knees. She hoped very much that Tom would be at home when she arrived.

17

WHEN MRS HARROW left the house Tom determined to follow her. He didn't really know why he wanted to do this but he knew that it was in some way important to him to find out whether after all she had this house she was talking about or whether it was all really a fantasy. Perhaps on the other hand it was a ruse for him to get away from his book especially as he wasn't quite clear what to do with Dixon, whom he was getting more and more to dislike if not actually to despise. It might have been that Dixon was becoming more and more unclear to him but he felt that it went deeper than that. Perhaps he felt that Dixon was a conman and he wanted to know if Mrs Harrow was a conwoman too.

He remembered the first time he had encountered her. It had been on the stair when he was going down with some rubbish to the bin, loaves of bread that he had forgotten about and had left lying about till they had become green, tins emptied of tasteless fruit, newspapers which he had now given up reading. She had been hanging up washing on the back green. Before he knew where he was she had begun to tell him about this new house that she was in the process of buying and decorating so that she could rent it to students and make money from it. She had told him that in the past she had been working in hotels. It seemed very important to her that he should know about her project, as if she felt that she wouldn't appear real to him or serious unless she had established herself as someone with a future and business to handle. He had been very bored, the bucket in his hand, she standing there small and squat with a cold fresh wind blowing about her. "The silly cow," he kept muttering to himself. She reminded him of a man called Derry he had met while he was working on the roads. This man was always writing away for jobs but when he was asked to go for an interview he never went. He wrote the letters very beautifully on fine notepaper and seemed quite educated. He kept the letters which he got back and showed them to anyone who would look at the evidence that in fact there was a possibility of his getting a job away from the roads. The very possibility was enough. The man was in fact Irish, always neatly turned out, and he wore a groomed moustache. He referred often to a small croft which he owned in Ireland and which he said he could go back to if he wished.

When therefore Mrs Harrow left the house dressed in her fragmentary furs, Tom followed her. He felt like a detective hired by some obscure agency to find out the truth about an evasive client. Some years before he would never have set on such a trial and he hardly even knew why he was doing it now. Mrs Harrow walked ahead of him quite briskly and he pursued her at a safe distance. She never looked back and he thought that this argued a definite purpose. Perhaps she really did have this house; perhaps she was really decorating it. They walked one behind the other across the windy bridge, her fur like the feathers of a bird stirred in the breeze.

All around him he could see signs of the city being rebuilt, old houses being pulled down, new ones going up. Yellow cranes like dinosaurs clawing at the earth. Men with acetylene lamps burning iron bars away, the blue flame flickering.

Eventually they reached the main part of the city and it was more difficult to keep track of her. She went into a super-market and he followed her, just keeping out of sight, as she pottered about with her wire basket, considering purchases and deciding against them, weighing their cost against her resources. He didn't know where her money came from, what she lived on. He thought that perhaps Ann would have known the answer to that sort of question without difficulty. Dixon, of course, wouldn't. She was too dumpy, too silly, too ordinary, for Dixon.

She paused for a long time at various counters. Once he saw her at the cheese counter, picking up cheeses and weighing them in her hand, as if deciding whether she was going to get value for money. Some were red and some white and some fat and fine and yellow in their cellophane covers. After a long time however she put them all down and turned away, not buying any of them after all. Ah, thought Tom laughingly, the tragedy of choice. The existentialist confrontations with cheese.

From the cheese counter she moved to the fruit counter and bought two oranges and some apples. Now and again she would look in her purse with an exact regard. It was funny to be watching another human being like this when she did not realise that she was being watched. There was something unclean about it. It reduced the person to a kind of machine, a caricature. It made him feel sordid. For a moment he nearly left the store.

When she eventually took the basket to the girl at the adding machine there was very little in it. Just the fruit, one or two tins, and a loaf. The girl didn't even look at her, she merely removed the articles from the basket and priced them on her machine. Music drifted over the supermarket, some pop song or other designed to soothe and prevent thought. Mrs Harrow walked out and he followed her. He was hoping she wouldn't get on a bus, but she made no move to do that. In any case it was dry and she probably didn't have much money.

She stopped for a long time at a jeweller's window and stared into it. There were rings, brooches, watches, stones of all kinds, emeralds, opals, etcetera. He couldn't imagine what she was thinking of as she stared dully at the window. Perhaps she was thinking of her marriage. Once she craned forward to look at a particularly large necklace of pearls which dangled and writhed on a red velvet background. She shifted the bag from one hand to another and moved on.

She went into the next shop which advertised ladies' clothes. He waited outside as he didn't dare to go in and hoped that there wasn't a back exit. Was this then how she spent her afternoons, going from shop to shop, studying the unattainable? He was stabbed by an almost unbearable pain. Why had he not known about this before? He saw coming towards him a dandyish looking man with grey hair and a grey moustache who was carrying a cane. The man reminded him of Dixon and he instantly disliked him. He thought, I shall get my revenge on Dixon for what he has done to me, for the fact that I believed in him. He thought of what he had heard one of the girls in the supermarket saying to a friend, "Do you know who I was dreaming of last night?"

"Go on, keep me in suspense," said the other girl.

"And it wasn't anyone I think much of," said the first girl. What did these girls have to do with Dixon or he with them? Tom thought, I don't like either of them.

A piece of paper swirled past him in a small whirlwind. He saw that it was a page out of a comic. Its cheap red vulgar paper delighted him so that for a moment he forgot that he was waiting and he nearly bent down and picked it up to read it.

She came out but she didn't see him. She continued on her way and he followed her. She went into a teashop and sat in a corner drinking tea and eating cake. She spent a long time there while he waited. Her back was to him and he could see her picking at the cake and drinking the tea delicately with her forefinger curled round the handle of the cup.

A policeman walked past him slowly turning his head this way and that. And Tom felt guilty as if he had been caught in some terrible act. But the policeman's glance bounced off him impersonally, calm and self-possessed. Still he himself had felt for a moment panicky as if he had been caught in another man's mind, and it shook him. Ahead of him on a corner he saw a small man with a wooden leg selling what must be artificial flowers. Now and again he would clasp his arms around his body. His face was thin and pale and indomitable. A thin slice of fat from the world's supermarket.

Mrs Harrow came out of the restaurant. He couldn't imagine where she was going next. She stopped for a moment at a huge cinema made of blue and white marble which was showing the *Decameron* and then passed on. As she walked ahead of him he tried to think what she must have been like in the past but couldn't. She might have been young and pretty but perhaps she hadn't been. She certainly must have been young. She walked on, clutching her bag, once patting her hair. Did she in fact do this pilgrimage every day? Was that how she passed the time?

Now she was standing at a bus stop. She was looking in her purse as if searching for her fare. In front of her was a man reading a newspaper. He thought: Perhaps she really has this house. Perhaps I should let her have it without investigation. But he wanted to know. One had heard of women leaving thousands of pounds after existing on bread and sausage in small dingy rooms. Perhaps she was one of them. Perhaps she was a genuine mystery and not to be ignored. As she stood at the bus stop the thought suddenly came to him that she looked rather like his mother if she had been a bit fatter. It was something about the stance, the stolid acceptance of what was to come. He shied away from the image.

The bus came and she climbed on it. It was almost for a moment as if she saw him but he couldn't be sure. Perhaps she had been aware of him the whole time, but he didn't think that. In any case it didn't matter, he wasn't yet ready to follow her to the ultimate conclusion. He was willing to let her have her house. The time for investigation hadn't yet come. Some time soon but not yet. It would be a terrible blow if the story weren't true. Somehow she had become important to him, with her moth-eaten fragmentary furs and her bag with the sparse foodstuffs. He felt he ought to give her a chance, but was that too a form of cowardice?

The bus drove away splashing him a bit as he stood there not caring whether she saw him or not. It occurred to him that when she came to him with jam and scones she was perhaps depriving herself of them and this made him feel uncomfortable, for it changed everything, didn't it?

He turned away from the bus stop and found himself face to face with a church. As he stood there, he saw people coming out of it. There had apparently been a wedding and they hung about in small groups talking self-consciously. In a short time Tom found himself in the middle of a group of spectators, mostly drab women with shopping bags, all standing by the railings, staring. He couldn't understand the expression on their faces. Perhaps it was a strange longing, perhaps a looking into a more romantic past which they had idealised, or into a possibility which had escaped them.

The bride, her white dress blossoming in the slight breeze, stood smiling nervously just outside the door. The tentative smile became more definite as a little boy wearing a kilt ran forward and offered her a bouquet of red flowers before retreating hastily into the shelter of his mother's arms. The bride held the bouquet uneasily as if it were a shopping bag. Her husband with oiled hair and a cut-price morning suit which seemed too large for him stood stiffly beside her. A photographer bent on one knee and fired his camera at them. The bride started as if she had been hit by a bullet and then resumed her shy, awkward, patient attitude.

The women gathered in groups around her, putting their hands on their hats as if they were in danger of blowing away. A small squat man with large red hands which he didn't seem to know what to do with stood beside the bride, probably her father. For the first time in his life Tom began to think about the ceremony as if from inside the mind of the bride. She was stepping out into a new world. She had taken a decision. She had decided to spend the rest of her days with that man with the oiled hair and the cut-price over-large suit. She had decided that she would have children by him and populate the world with miniature versions of the two of them. This was in fact the greatest day of her life, the only day in her whole life that people would stop and stare at her as if she were some bird clad in common yet extraordinary plumage. The only day on which she would emerge from the crowd, the only day she would be famous.

She would keep the photographs, she would remember those people who had been at her wedding, she would remember that day with its slight breeze, she might even remember Tom as a face she had once seen. She would think of herself as fresh and blossoming. Tom thought with amazement that once upon a time, on perhaps such a day, his own father and mother had been like this, they too had made a decision about each other, they too had worn their new strange clothes, they too had thought that the world was beginning anew. His mother had smiled exactly like this, shyly and nervously, his father had stood there awkwardly perhaps in such an over-large suit. The two of them had made a decision in the real world.

For this was a real thing, it was not fictional. It was not a dream. This was a stepping out into the flux, which would be renewed forever by an album of coloured photographs. The two of them would become "one flesh". This was a ceremony to which all must conform except the saints and the hermits and the neurotic. She must take on the responsibility of the real world. The mother, who looked clumsy and ill-dressed, must look after the guests, she must send out invitations, she must do everything in the way it was done by everybody else. The bride too must do things in the right way, she must cut the cake, she must buy the right sort of dress. It was amazing how all those things got done. They got done because they were necessary.

It was amazing how "ordinary" people did these right things, how they learned to do them. They did not live in a world of fiction, they allowed things to be what they were, they did not probe and dissect them, they did not create phantoms and gargoyles and monsters. They rested in the real. They learned how to see about the minister and pay him, how the right people must be seated at the right tables, how the telegrams must be read. He felt it extraordinary that all this should happen in such a fluent way. And yet they all appeared ordinary and drab. And all the people around him knew this too, they too had undergone it all. They had succeeded in being married and marrying. They had taken on responsibility.

Taxis began to appear and the people left the church and entered them, talking animatedly. They would go to a cheap hotel somewhere and have their fairly cheap food and every-thing would be done correctly.

The spectators too began to drift away and he was left alone. Without knowing what he was doing he went into the church. He stared straight down the aisle and saw that at the organ a white-haired man was playing by himself as if unaware that everyone had gone. The music he was playing didn't sound like a hymn tune, it seemed classical. Perhaps it was Bach or someone like that. He stayed for some time listening to the music and watching the player who hadn't noticed him, then he went out again. Perhaps the organist was a purist, he played for himself alone. Perhaps he liked playing without an audience. Perhaps that was what his purity consisted of.

He entered a pub and ordered a beer.

He drank steadily. For some reason the white-haired man playing alone haunted him. He seemed to be symbolic of something though he couldn't tell what. The white helpless hair had seemed to drift down the back of his head as in a picture of Beethoven he had once seen.

"As a matter of fact," said a woman who was sitting at the next table, "he had no reason to be jealous . . ."

Tom went to the bar and leaned on it ordering a whisky. He felt reckless as if he wanted to spend all his money. The man beside him was reading a sports paper.

"To tell you the truth," said the man to the barman, "I didn't think Johnstone played so well last Saturday. I think he's past it."

"I'll tell you something," said the barman leaning forward confidentially, "I'll tell you something. European football is far better than ours."

"I agree," said the man.

"I'll tell you," the barman continued, "if I was managing the Scottish team I'll tell you what I'd do. I'd teach them to control the ball, and how to pass. That's where the Europeans have it over us all the time, all the time."

"Couldn't agree more," said Sports Paper. "Couldn't agree more. Our players can't pass. Not inch-perfect passes."

"And what's more—" said the barman. "Another whisky, sir?" he said to Tom.

"And what's more," he continued after pouring it out, "they can pass moving forward, that's what they can do. I'd have them out hail and shine, passing and controlling the ball. That's what I'd do."

"No doubt about it," said Sports Paper, "I agree a hundred per cent. A hundred per cent. Jim Baxter could do that, I think you'll agree."

"Jim Baxter . . ." said the barman, sighing. "We'll never see his likes again, I can tell you that right now. We'll never see another Jim Baxter, that's for sure. And I'll tell you something else. My father used to tell me that Alan Morton could do it. But nowadays what do you get? What do you get? You get people who kick the ball up the park and hope for the best. That's what you get. They kick it up the park."

"I agree absolutely," said Sports Paper. "No question of it. That's what they do. That's why people won't go and watch them. That's why the League is folding up."

"You can say that again," said the barman wiping the bar busily with a cloth. "At his best Johnstone is good I grant you but he's never been any good in an international. He's too moody, that's what's wrong with him. Gordon Smith was the same, he was never any good in an international. I grant you he was good for his club but not in an international. In an international, never."

"You never said a truer word," said Sports Paper, "never a truer word."

"And I'll tell you something else—" said the barman.

"Another whisky, sir? And I'll tell you something else, till they get the players to control the ball they'll never get anywhere against the Continental sides. Nowhere. We've got the talent but what do we do with it? We waste it. They'll have to start from basics, that's what I say. We should be out all the time looking for youngsters, that's what the scouts should be doing. Right?"

"Right," said Sports Paper.

Much later Tom walked home in the cold air. He felt light-headed. The city around him was vibrating and blazing with lights. It was dangerous and precarious. In the distance he could see the multi-storey flats remote and cold like banks of computers. He tried to imagine what it would be like to live in one of them, problems of milk and mail, all sorts of daily problems, or standing at the window on a summer's morning high as the birds and looking out across the river. But at night they looked like the latest in technology, all green lights, shining above the huddled slums, with their rustlings of rats.

What was Dixon doing now? Writing away somewhere in his airy flat. Fitting his masterpiece together. Far from the madding crowd. Wearing his bow tie, playing his music, putting his ironies on the record player.

Tom felt as if he wanted to talk to someone. He would have to go back to his flat and continue with his own book, such as it was. There was nothing else he could do. Even though he hated his hero now. Even though he couldn't stand him. And ahead of him another mile of walking in the cold night in the pulsing city.

As he walked along, for the first time in his life he felt afraid. He had to cross the windy bridge and he was panicking. He stopped for a moment. He couldn't understand the sudden panic, why he was suddenly shaking, why his whole body seemed to be vibrating like the bridge in a high wind. He stopped as if to gather himself together before proceeding. It wasn't altogether that he was drunk. He wasn't drunk, only light-headed. It was almost as if he felt that he didn't exist, as if he was a shade, a ghost, a coloured ripple on the water. He was a frightened shade. The book was slipping away from him, he realised, and the book had been his reason for existence. Dixon was fading away from him, with his twisted ironical superior smile, he could see him drifting into the complex of lights, into the winds. He could feel him leaking away from him, whole paragraphs, chapters.

His feet echoed on the bridge and as he walked along he saw for the first time a figure coming towards him. The figure was black and carrying something in its hand. He thought it might be a knife but surely it couldn't be that. I shall run, he thought, I shall run away. I shall turn back. There was the bridge shaking in the wind and the water below. Never before had he felt so frightened. He knew that the figure was hostile. He knew that he was going to be attacked. And yet he was advancing towards the figure. Slowly, but still advancing. And after all he had very little money. His feet rang on the stone as he walked into the wind towards the black figure. What was frightening him? He couldn't understand it. He had never been so conscious of his body before, of his bones, of his blood, of his flesh, of his vulnerability. But now he was conscious of them. He felt them as distinct and heavy, his own and not his own. He felt the blood tingling in his body. He felt himself as mortal, his bared breast, his bared face.

The black figure was coming towards him. And he knew that he must go forward or die. The wind shook them both but the figure hadn't stopped, it was coming on, a ballet dancer. In the terrible opera of lights. The wind was pure and piercing and screaming. His legs dragged him forward against his will since every other part of him wanted to run back. And at a certain point across the bridge he surrendered. His body seemed to say, let what will happen happen. And then at that very moment a warmth coursed through him, a fire, his body became fiercely pure and exhilarated. His feet moved freely forward, he didn't care. He was willing to let it all happen, all the events that would happen. He felt them as necessary. He would remember that night for the rest of his life. Ahead of him was the killer—he knew there were many of these attackers—but his body had decided it didn't care. His body had decided, let what will happen happen. And as it did so he felt free. He felt as if he could dance. Some energy was released in him. The city blazed around him with marvellous beauty, heartbreaking in the pure desert wind.

And as he came up to the figure he saw that after all it was a man in a black suit carrying a rolled up umbrella which he could not unfurl in the wind. The man looked at him terrified and he looked back. He said, "Good evening", and walked on. For a moment Tom had a sense of a transformation, a magical renewal, as if really there had been a killer there and by simply going forward he had changed the killer into a peaceable man with an umbrella. It had been like something out of a fairy tale. Suddenly he danced gaily and shouted into the teeth of the wind as if he had discovered himself. Suddenly he was filled with an overwhelming joy, suddenly he heard in the voices of the wind extraordinary hopes, and smelt real perfumes. Suddenly he felt that he could write good things, that he could create a chapter which would burn with pure fire and which would have the desert wind howling in it. And he realised that the bridge was long passed and he was near home.

18

THE SCHOOL WAS large and airy and full of glass and it was built on a slight rise on a hill out of the city. Tom asked the janitor where Ann's room was and was directed across the hall into an alcove where he found it. He knocked on the door. She didn't seem at all surprised to see him and she asked him to come in. Some children dressed up in bright clothes were standing about on the floor as if they had been taking part in a play. She introduced him to them as a gentleman who would like to see them acting and they considered this to be quite natural and continued with what they were doing. After a while he realised that the play was *Cinderella*.

In the first scene there was Cinderella herself, dressed in a drab gown, scrubbing the floor with the back of a duster while she carried the wastepaper basket about with her to do duty for a bucket. Lolling on chairs with pieces of chalk in their mouths were the two ugly sisters who weren't in fact at all ugly. They gossiped to each other while now and again throwing instructions at Cinderella who dashed about making imaginary beds, cleaning the floor, bringing in coal and so on.

Then a little boy came in with an envelope, which was supposed to contain the invitation to the ball. The two sisters squabbled over it and started to dress up, making Cinderella comb their hair and attend to their clothes. The glass in the door served as a mirror. The two ugly sisters were enchanting blonde girls with long hair who however spoke peevishly and harshly as if echoing the language of their parents. They stamped their feet and shouted and screamed with adult authority and shortly afterwards gossiped to each other about the ball. He found their ability to make such transitions quite extraordinary.

The two sisters left and Cinderella was left alone. She sat down miserably at a desk which had been drawn out to the middle of the floor and talked tearfully to herself. She heard a sound, looked up, and was confronted by her Fairy Godmother in a ballooning white dress, waving a ruler for a wand and repeating the age-old magical words in an endearing childish voice.

"Who are you?" she said in a faltering voice.

"I am your Fairy Godmother."

There was the business with the coach and horses and the pumpkins. Tom marvelled at the assurance and inventiveness of the children. For instance, instead of pumpkins they had oranges.

Cinderella was transformed and set off for the ball.

The next scene was the ball. Dancers danced together to pop music. The children had picked up impeccably the mannerisms of the dancers on *Top of the Pops* and swayed with a cool sensuousness to the record. They were inexpressibly poignant, their childlike bodies merging into an adult poise. At one side of the room was the prince and his attendant—a fat boy with a running nose—talking to each other in a superior manner. Standing on the other side were the two ugly sisters, making malicious comments about the dancers, and waving petulant fans. They rolled their eyes and sighed in an exaggerated manner. At one stage they each in turn asked the prince for a dance but he turned away disdainfully, and gazed at a map of Scotland which hung on the wall.

Then Cinderella entered, dressed in white. He went over to her and they danced. One by one the dancers all dropped away leaving the two dancers in the middle of the floor. Suddenly a little girl rushed out and moved the hands of the clock to midnight. Cinderella gathered her dress about her and rushed off, leaving her shoe behind her. The prince ran out the door, looked this way and that, apparently couldn't see her and came back disconsolately.

In the third scene the two sisters were discussing the ball when there was a knock at the door. It was the prince and his servant. They asked if the sisters could try on a shoe which the servant was carrying. They did so eagerly, squabbling with each other when they heard what it was for, but the shoe fitted neither. In another part of the room, though really off stage, Cinderella was sitting on the floor, listening to sad music from a record player. The prince asked the sisters if there was anyone else in the house but they assured him there was no one. He asked where the music was coming from. They made all sorts of excuses but eventually he demanded to see where the music was coming from and Cinderella was brought on to the stage. He tried the shoe on her foot and it fitted. It was really the girl he had seen at the ball though she was in fact dressed in dull grey.

The wedding took place to pop music, comic and yet somehow moving. Tom noticed how the girl who had been acting the part of Cinderella seemed to have projected herself into the world of a princess: there was a grace about her movements, a conscious pride. He was astonished at the ideas and turmoil that seethed in his own head. He had never realised that education could be like this, that it could draw from children this spontaneous commitment. The atmosphere of the class was warm, free and relaxed. There was a feeling of emotional growth in the air, a controlled unpredictability. The fact that there was no script seemed to help. And all the time Ann was standing in the background, except that now and then she would interject an idea if the play was settling into a repetitive groove. He gazed at her in astonishment realising that she was a craftsman, a real teacher. And yet to look at her one would not have believed this. She looked usually so pale and quiet but here she was changed, had become strangely beautiful.

When the play was over and the bell had rung and the children had left for their lunch he said to her :

"That was amazing."

"You liked it then?" She seemed pleased.

"It was superb," he said. "Absolutely. I didn't think that sort of thing was possible."

"Oh, anything is possible. What you have to do is release their energies. That's all. They are natural actors."

There was an awkward silence and then she said, "Would you like to see around for a bit?"

They walked around and they looked at drawings and paintings. They saw magazines and newspapers lying about on desks. They saw piles of bright books, crayons, tape-recorders, record players. The paintings on the walls, she told him, were by the children themselves. Everywhere were bright colours, a higgledy piggledy storm of creativity, as if ideas were being picked out of the air in accordance with the laws of life itself. There was no sense of a forced order, no sense of anyone looking for a theology that would unite the data, that would arrange the world. Everything incomplete, disorderly, spawning . . .

"It's quite astonishing," he said. "Astonishing." He felt as if he had encountered something important, as if he had been hit on the head with a hammer which made bright colours fly around him.

"I found your note," he said at last. "It was inside the door when I got home."

"Yes, I went to your flat but you weren't there," she said. She didn't tell him about her feeling of desolation when he hadn't answered the door.

"There was a man with a dog," she said. "The dog was leaping up at him all the time. It was very odd."

"Yes," he said, "one of these days it'll bite him." He was suddenly awkward again and couldn't think what to say. She looked so at home where she was, and so suddenly desirable, because she knew what she was doing with her life. She seemed to have a purpose and to be inside that purpose, surrounded by her own kind of creativity, and the idea of it staggered him for a moment. Perhaps, he thought, she is more creative than me. And he was puzzled by the thought, as if suddenly he had been pushed off an imaginary rock.

"Is there anywhere you want to go," he said.

"Why don't we go out of the city on Monday?" she said. "We have a holiday."

"I'd like that," he said.

He was enthusiastic about his idea. "We could go into the country. We could take a bus and walk about and come back at night. It might be a good day."

"I would really like that," she said.

She looked at her watch. "I must go for my lunch," she said. "I have to go to the canteen. I'll see you on Monday then."

"Come to the flat then," he said. "We'll leave from the flat. At about two o'clock."

"All right," she said. As she turned away he gazed after her for a while. Her trim figure disappeared round a corner and he turned away from the room with all its projects and bright paintings. He went out of the school threading his way between bunches of shouting children who were running about as if demented in their world. There was a fresh breeze blowing and he felt as if he were moving with it, as if sails inside him were filling with it, and there was a blue glittering sea ahead of him.

19

Dixon couldn't make up his mind whether Sheila was what he wanted after all. Most of the time since he had come to the flat he felt suspended in space, and he wasn't making much headway with the book. It was disquieting that the barbarians were beginning to appear more real than his heroine who was supposed to represent the values of culture and elitism. They haunted his dreams with their hairy bodies, their terrifying energies, their monstrous and broken urgent speech. They emerged out of the forest circling the White City with its white vulnerable spires. They sang strange seductive songs. Their skins were black as if they had come from Hades with their strange swaying music.

Sometimes he seemed to be wholly seduced by their songs, their innocent, childlike, brutal ways. But Sheila did not belong to their world. She belonged to a well-mannered, moral world. His heroine had changed a lot since he had started on the book. At first she had been energetic and barbaric herself, but now she was becoming purer and more helplessly female. And as this happened so there were arising in his own breast solitary beastlike feelings as if he wished to destroy the world which had reared him, in which he had once believed, so that he wished to appear at the White City with banners on which were scrawled not Latin mottoes of noble aspirations but obscenities such as one might find scrawled on lavatory walls.

Was it that he was missing his wife with her harsh bitter ways? Was it that she was needed for a certain tension that

*his work required? Had he made a mistake in leaving her?
Sometimes he would pace up and down his room at night
staring despairingly at his typewriter, its rows of teeth. What
challenge did he need? He felt as if he were hurling himself
against space and not solidity. Could he exist without his
wife's ignorant asperities? He didn't know. Could he exist at
all? Did he exist at all?*

*The City with the White Spires became more and more
unreal, the barbarians approached closer and closer. One
night he had a terrible dream. It was of an animal that
looked like a cat. As it lay on a carpet in a strange house
which he didn't recognise, it slowly ate a snake which was
lying in front of it. Its body rippled with the effort of
swallowing, and then it voided the snake through its back
passage and began to eat it again. He watched the endless
process with fascination and fear. He knew it had something
to do with his book and his life. The white towers were
becoming more and more corpselike and dim. Their museums
and libraries were fading away into the darkness and he did
not have enough energy in himself to keep them standing
solidly and meaningfully. He even stopped reading books.
At first he had gone to the bookshops to browse about when
he wasn't writing but he had ceased to do that. He studied
his own work and found it inadequate. He was growing
bored with his book. It didn't seem to mesh with the
machinery of reality. It was like a diseased plant that was
growing in an air of its own. The book belonged to the
doomed City of the White Spires. He had impulses at night
to leave his room and plunge into the destructive darkness
where the illuminated sharks cruised, and the lost people
stared dully down at the pavement. He wanted to forget
himself, his mind, its tortures and terrors. The mind was
becoming too much of a responsibility.*

He wondered what was happening out in the city at night. Did he want to save himself or go out into its darkness to be destroyed? Did he want to feel the teeth in his throat for the last time? He had never felt such contradictions before. Perhaps they were a sign of failing powers? On the other hand perhaps they might be the beginnings of a new creative pain and excitement? Should he return to his wife, to her sharp, silly, biting ways? Would that save him or was he too late for that? He had hidden himself away and he didn't know where he was. What darkness was creeping over him, what eclipse was steadily covering the distant whiteness of his mind? A pure high note was singing somewhere, steadily coming closer like the sound of the siren of a fire engine. But where was the fire? And where were the busy people with their red helmets making for?

Sometimes he had nightmares as if he himself were on fire in the darkness where the blaze of the sun had gone out. Sometimes he was even drawn to the works of Nietzsche which he had in his bookcase, but he couldn't summon up enough energy to read them.

One day he took Sheila to the zoo as they had arranged. In any case there weren't many places he could think of to take her to.

They had looked into the cages where the chimpanzees, wearing their muddy gloves, had scratched themselves for fleas. They had seen the lions and tigers pacing up and down, the ugly, busy wolverines, the pumas with their contented deadly gaze. They had seen the tropical birds, and the pheasants in their glowing stained glass colours. The baboons swung from bar to bar with an agility faster than the eye could follow. The crocodile slept like a log, scarcely breathing.

In one cage a black vulture stared downwards at its mess

of meat. The deer and the antelope grazed peacefully, the llamas looked huge against the sky and the penguins waddled up and down in their white and red.

She had walked beside him in her brown coat, looking, as usual, quiet and composed.

Once he had stood as if in a dream studying a tiger which paced to and fro without ceasing, attracted by the power and compactness of its body. Its eyes glanced at him indifferently. He had a sudden impulse to open all the cages and let all the animals out into the breezy chilly day. Let them destroy, let them redeem.

He said this aloud and she looked at him, horror-stricken. "That would be a terrible thing," she said. But he had a vision of the animals clawing, leaping, diving, springing lithely and elegantly at the people with their bags of crisps, their vacant eyes, across which the animals moved in a cinema which had come to life.

And as he looked at her he was filled with an overpowering sadness whose source he could not locate.

His own writing didn't have any animal power, he realised, it was merely a phantasm, a reflection casting shadows behind it and not ahead. He felt a vast hot alien sun at the back of his head and was terrified for a moment lest his head itself might be that sun.

She put her hand into his as if she had felt some of that piercing perplexity. Above them in the breezy sky the name-less clouds endlessly passed. He looked down at her protect-ively. She looked like a small timid animal in her brown coat.

"I'm all right," he said at last, watching the restaurant ahead of him with its advertisements for Coca Cola. I need to be saved, he thought. There is some place that I need to get to.

The animals at which they had gazed—even the wildcats

—looked so playful and so innocent. How could one believe in their destructive power, their undeviating remorseless chasing of the wounded and the helpless, the lion's jaw sunk in the striped zebra? Yet how amiably the lion blinked as he drowsed in the sun.

The eagle brooding on its perch, the hawk, how could one understand their instant unperplexed power? Sheila stared at him in bewilderment as if she did not understand him either. And yet he was no eagle, no panther, no tiger.

They left the zoo and went for tea in a large draughty restaurant. He looked at her for a long time across the table with its cracked marble surface, without being able to say anything. Once he put his hand to his head as if he had a headache. But it was his whole being that was aching, his whole soul.

"Drink your tea," he said at last. But he was thinking of the animals in their cages pacing up and down, endless caged storms. He was imagining what the storms would be like if they were released . . .

Tom couldn't fix an exact time at which he had begun to hate Dixon. It seemed to have grown on him slowly, the feeling of hate and disgust. At first he had admired him for his aristocratic ease, his air of aloof confident hauteur, his expertise. He envied his vast study with its marble busts, his resources of learning, knowledge of music. He admired him for his mind, its white cold light, its knowledge of Europe and the past. He associated him with wit and grace and leisure. He associated him with music and flowers and paintings. And gradually he began to hate him.

He hated him really because he was inhuman and brittle. He realised that there was nothing that Dixon had ever really loved, not with any depth, not for itself alone. At the beginning he had thought that Dixon had never felt anger or envy or jealousy. He was an Olympian. And because he had begun to hate him he set out to destroy him. He resolved that Dixon had been given enough of unearned light. Now he must be punished. He must be smashed into little bits and if possible reassembled. He wanted to destroy Dixon before Dixon destroyed him.

At first he didn't realise that he was involved in a life and death struggle with Dixon. After all Dixon was only a fictitious character. But as time passed he sensed, instinctively as a cobra confronted by a mongoose does, that this was a fight to the finish, that one of them must die. Art was not a matter of looking at Parozone bottles.

And he began to grow afraid of Dixon. He began to grow

afraid that Dixon was getting out of control. Something terrible was entering his own writing, as for instance in the chapter he had written about the zoo. His writing had not frightened him before. It was something that he did which he remained detached from. It was something that he sat down to as he might sit down to tea. But it was becoming different. It was becoming stained and distorted by life, it was releasing a devil. It was as if the acid in the bottle of Parozone had been released and was burning his hand. Dixon had become a Mephistopheles in bow tie and dancing suit, a question mark posed by a witty con-man, an enigma, a desperate joke. One of them would have to be killed as in a Western. One of them would have to fall on the street on both sides of which stood the gimcrack brittle houses. But which one? And where would the bullet come from? He saw the two of them walking slowly towards each other down a street while the crooked judge and the frightened proles ran for cover, peeping out between the curtains of wooden houses. But he didn't know which one of them would drop. Which would succumb to the reality of the bullet on the flimsy set?

His hatred of Dixon grew. He thought of sending him back to his wife but it was too late for that. He thought he should send him out from his flat on to the streets late at night to die in a knife fight, coming across the bridge at night, at a time when an umbrella would turn into a sword. Dixon was dangerous, he knew that now. But then the more dangerous Dixon grew the better, perhaps, might grow his own writing. That was the paradox. Dixon was pushing him into a corner. Did he want to go into that corner?

Should he let the animals out of their cages? But if they attacked Dixon would they attack him as well? The man in the white suit must die, the piranha must eat the flesh from his bones in the stormy river into which he would be pitched. The man dedicated to the marble and the green leaf must die. There was no way out. But if Dixon were to die what would happen to himself, that is, Tom Spence? That was the question and the paradox. For perhaps he himself was dependent on Dixon in a weird symbiosis. Still, he was determined that he would die, that he would suffer . . .

21

Tʜᴇʏ ᴡᴀʟᴋᴇᴅ ᴛᴏɢᴇᴛʜᴇʀ in the wood, while, along the main road, not far away, cars whizzed past and Tom wished for a moment that one or other of them had a car. They had come by bus to where they were. Tom liked being back among "nature" again and so did she, though neither of them had much detailed knowledge of it and did not know the names of the trees. Tom looked about to see if there were any live animals anywhere but could only see some sheep higher up among some stony hills. The only sound to be heard was made by a stream which flowed along among logs and through marshy ground.

"You know of course," he said suddenly, his lips pouting like a child's, "that I don't have any money."

She didn't say anything but smiled. Looking at her he knew that they were together, that some intimacy had grown between the two of them, and that there was a possibility of their being together always. He felt relaxed and happy and jumped across the stream instead of looking for an easy crossing. He had completely forgotten about his book—all books—feeling that he was among real things.

"I used to work cutting down trees," he boasted.

"Oh?" she said without surprise. She too looked happy, gazing up at the bare trees and down at the ground as if she were expecting to see some interesting vegetation or animals. He wondered whether she was thinking about another project.

"And I did other jobs as well. I used to work at the post

office." He felt that he could tell her the story about the wheelbarrow, and this surprised him since he was rather ashamed of it and hadn't spoken about it to anyone before. But he didn't actually tell her.

"I think you should go in for teaching," she said casually. "I think you would be very good. You could get a grant."

Surprisingly he heard himself saying in a light tone, "I'll think about it."

"I think you would be quite good," she said again. A bird passed overhead, a small bird with a golden breast, but he didn't know its name. He felt at home among the trees, they appealed to something secretive in his nature, and yet he was irritated that he knew so little. Why did he know so little about the world, he wondered.

"Funny," he said, stopping and looking at her. "I don't know anything about anything. All I've ever done is labouring and delivering letters. I don't know the names of anything here. I can type but not much else. Other people can do so many things. I'm really an ignorant sod. What can you do?"

She laughed. "I can cook," she said. "I teach. And that's about all. Oh, I can decorate a house. I've done that."

"I've never done that," he said resentfully. "I've never done anything. Still, I've got over fifty pounds left. It'll last me a while yet, and then I'll have to find a job again."

"I've got some money," she said.

"I wouldn't touch it. Look here." He was gazing at a beetle which was crawling along a log. It shone bluely in the daylight and moved very slowly.

"I think that's a beetle," he said, glad to have recognised something in the wood.

But he felt that sometimes they weren't talking to each other at all, they were disguising themselves from each other.

She was standing there in her brown coat and he in his khaki coat because the day was cold, but they weren't really two people talking to each other. He would have to find a way to talk to her, he would have to become desperate enough. There was a part of him, he knew, that he was holding back, and this holding back came from pride. He had never really talked to women, not even to his mother who had ordered him about and who was continually asking him, "Have you passed your exams?" She wasn't interested in him at all, she was only concerned with him in so far as he was a projection of her own desires.

In the far distance he could see some hills with snow on them. He remembered once passing a farm and seeing a farmer feeding hens. Among them was a large goose which suddenly raised its towering neck and cackled furiously at the ring of white hills. Among the warm domestic hens and the farmer in his muddy wellingtons it looked remote and cold and almost eerie.

He helped her across another small stream and found that her hand remained in his. For a moment he was astonished, it had remained there with such confidence and ease. It was like receiving an electric shock or touching frosted steel. He fell silent and she didn't speak either. They walked on, picking their steps carefully. The wood darkened about them and then lightened again. They came out on to a field and saw some cows grazing. A single horse stood by itself staring out at nothing, its back against a rusty fence. Far beyond he could see a black bull standing perfectly still as if made of marble.

He stopped when he saw a snail below him. It was black and its horns jutted out. He knelt down and placed his hand on the ground in front of it to see what it would do. Would it be conscious of him? He said playfully to Ann, "If it turns aside I will go in for a proper job." She smiled mildly down at him. She knew that they wouldn't be parted now. It was something childlike in him that attracted her, an echo of her teaching. She saw him as a little boy, playing in the wide world. She thought, I can change him and there won't be anyone else but us. Suddenly he shouted, "It turned away. It must have sensed me. Isn't that odd?"

"What will we do if it rains?" she said. "We're out in the wilderness here." There was nothing but roots, shapeless roots, and tall trees, bare and smooth.

But she felt secure simply because there was another person there. She hadn't realised how lonely she had been. She didn't think that Tom was greatly talented, she didn't think of him at all in that way. Perhaps he thought he was talented but she thought of him as a small boy who needed to be looked after. Her mind wasn't stormy. She wasn't really interested in literature. She was content with what she saw around her.

He was standing facing her pointing a branch at her. She was startled to see his imitation of a soldier with a gun. "Get a move on," he shouted joyfully in a German voice. "Ve hav vays of making you talk." And then he burst out laughing. He imagined the wood as dangerous, and himself a commando or something like that. And she thought, the wood is dangerous. Only we haven't suffered enough. We haven't suffered at all. We have been privileged in spite of everything. We can walk about without guns being pointed at us, without being under surveillance.

"Don't be so silly," she said tolerantly.

"Do you think I should give up my writing?" he said, still pointing the bare leafless branch at her.

"Of course not," she said. "What a silly thing to say. Only you can say that."

In fact she would like him to carry on with his writing. But he should also get a job. One could do both. Surely that was possible.

"I wonder if there are any weasels in the wood," he said suddenly. "Or rats." He went on, "I've never seen a weasel. It's supposed to be very dangerous, ruthless. It's supposed to kill for the sake of killing." He brought out this scrap of natural knowledge with a certain pride.

"I didn't know that," she said.

As they were walking along her shoe caught in a hole and she said, "Help me out." He came over and untwisted her shoe free. "Are you all right?" he asked, his face concerned.

"I think so."

He pulled her up, and as he did so he looked into her eyes, and at that moment without thinking they kissed each other for the first time. It wasn't a violent kiss, it was a safe secure kiss. She closed her eyes and then after a while opened them. He was looking down at her with eyes open and as he saw her eyes opening he laughed. They both laughed and she drew herself gently away.

They walked along the road hand in hand. As they reached it he suddenly said, "Do you know what? There's a hotel near here. We'll go there. It's quite near and we can walk. We won't need the bus. It's quite a large hotel. We'll be there about five. I've got enough money to get us some food."

"I've got five pounds," she said.

They walked along the grassy verge of the road while the cars whizzed past: for not the first time he wished he had a car, but on the other hand it was good to be walking in the clear, fresh, slightly chill air.

After some time they came to a drive and at the end of it they saw a large building which Tom said was the hotel.

There weren't many people about and they eventually found the bar, which was open though there was no one in attendance. There was an imitation fire which simmered with red flames without heat, and on the walls were crossed dirks and claymores and, set in one wall, small windows glazed in various colours in which red, blue and purple predominated. They sat down on the easy chairs and waited for someone to arrive.

"They have a dance tonight," said Ann looking at a poster straight ahead of her.

"I see that," said Tom. He was taking out his wallet to see how much money he had with him.

"It's all right," said Ann, "I've got enough."

"No, I'll pay," said Tom. He felt suddenly reckless as if he wanted to stay there all night and his mind was perfectly clear after his walk.

Shortly afterwards a girl in a short red kilt served them their drinks. Tom took whisky neat and Ann a shandy.

"Nice place," he said looking round him. "It'll get busy later on."

"I'm sure," said Ann.

She had taken off her coat and felt slightly cold.

"Tell you what," said Tom with enthusiasm, "we'll have dinner here. Why not? I've got plenty of money."

"But dinner won't be till seven or half past six," said Ann. "That's an hour and a half away."

"It doesn't matter," said Tom, "we'll drink till then. We don't need to drink much but we can drink something. We don't need to get drunk."

At that moment two young lads dressed in checked shirts who looked as if they had been skiing came in. They ordered drinks and sat down at an adjacent table.

"I suppose there will be some skiing around here," said Ann.

"Yes, I think so," said Tom. One of the boys had startlingly fair, almost white, hair, and the other had black hair. They looked attractive and fresh and young and competent.

Ann smiled at one of them after he had spilt some of his drink on the table and he nodded his head pleasantly and then resumed talking with his friend.

"I'll go and get a menu," said Tom.

He walked along a very long corridor and came to the dining room which was at the far end. It was set out with spotlessly white tablecloths, and pictures of deer and blue hills all round the walls. He was given a menu by a stout cheerful woman and he went back.

He found Ann talking to the two boys. She was asking them if it had been cold on the hills and the fair one was describing a fall which he considered comic. Tom went over and bought himself a whisky; Ann still had some of her shandy left. He sat down at the table with his back to the two boys and Ann stopped talking to them. He thought she looked very pretty after her walk. There was a lot of colour in her cheeks and she looked vivacious and happy.

"I'm glad we came," she said. "I like this place."

"If you'd like to dance," he said, "I'll stay and watch you. I don't dance, but if you'd like to."

"We'll see," she said happily. He was glad that she was enjoying herself but at the back of his mind was a shadow about the two boys. He wished he could ski or do something interesting or dramatic. He wished there was something they could do together so that they could talk about it, a purpose achieved happily in the fresh air.

A tall man in dark glasses came in and stood by the bar.

He was wearing a red anorak and looking around him as he drank his whisky. There was about him an air of confidence and negligence as if he had plenty of money and knew his way around. He talked easily to the barmaid as if he was in the habit of coming there often, though it was clearly an expensive hotel. He talked loudly and mentioned a boat which he apparently owned. He also mentioned something about cheques. Tom hated him on sight. He didn't like the way in which he spoke out loud as if he assumed that his concerns, his life, were important to other people.

He and Ann drank quietly without saying much. Suddenly Tom said:

"I've been thinking about what you said about teaching. I'll think it over."

Ann seemed to waken out of a dream:

"Oh, of course I did say that, didn't I?"

"You did, a few times," said Tom suddenly angry. He couldn't understand why he was so angry; perhaps it was something to do with the two boys and the man, perhaps it had to do with feeling slightly out of place in these surroundings where one needed a cheque book or a boat or skis.

"I'm sorry. I was thinking about something else," said Ann.

"What? What were you thinking of?"

"Oh, nothing in particular."

"I see."

"I'll tell you what it was. I was thinking that I could do a project on hotels. Role playing, you know. Hotels from day to day."

"That would be nice," said Tom without enthusiasm.

The place was beginning to fill up. Handsome, rich-looking men with their well-dressed aristocratic girl friends were coming in. They all looked easy and suave as if accustomed to hotels of this quality and seemed to be talking about boats or skis.

"Oh, I'm sorry," said Tom, "I left the menu on the bar. I'll go and get it." He did so and they studied it together.

"It looks very expensive," said Ann. "Are you sure you want to have dinner?"

"We came here to have a night out," said Tom, "and that's what we'll do." But certainly it looked as if dinner would cost them two pounds each.

"I think I'll have the melon," said Ann. "I won't have the soup."

"And I think I'll have the soup," said Tom. "I feel quite cold. Do you feel cold?"

"Not now. I did at first. But not now."

Tom felt in the mood for showing off, spending all the money he had. "Would you like another shandy?" he said. "I'll have a whisky." Before she could reply he went over and bought both, thrusting his way through the crush. After the whisky he felt pleasantly warm and thought he would drink all night. He didn't care whether all his money gave out or not.

He noticed as he sat down that the fair-haired boy was smiling at Ann though she looked away when he sat down. He didn't say anything but drank his whisky. Someone at the far end of the room was playing on a guitar the tune of *California*. After that he played *Waly Waly*.

"That's my favourite tune," said Tom and he began to recite the ballad very quietly in her ear.

> O waly waly gin love be bonny
> A little time ere it is new
> but when 'tis auld it waxeth cauld
> and fades awa like the morning dew.

150

"It's very beautiful," said Ann.

"There are many more verses," said Tom. There was nothing like the ballads. Their bareness and beauty. He hummed under his breath :

O had I wist before I kist
that love had been sae hard to win
I'd hae locked my hert in a case of gowd
and pinned it wi' a siller pin.

Suddenly for the first time in his life he was pierced by the most bitter pain he had ever experienced. It was partly seeing Ann sitting so pensively in profile and humming the tune. In some strange manner the two came together and he realised that he loved her and that if he lost her he would be ruined. It was amazingly simple and amazingly frightening. So terrified was he that his hand with the whisky glass shook and went on shaking and he stared down at it in astonishment. The pain in his breast was bitter and bare and bleak like the pain in the ballads and he felt for the first time in his life, as distinct from knowing, exactly what the girl in the ballad had felt, her hopelessness, her desolation. The bar seemed to swing round him in slow motion as if he were drunk but he knew he wasn't drunk, it was something else, some piercing pain that was wholly irrational and irrevocable.

"I think," he said aloud, "you're very pretty." He wanted to touch her, to stroke her hair, but he didn't.

"Thank you," she replied without any hint of coquetry. She felt warm and cosy. She liked hearing people sing, she liked to be among people. Tom got up and bought another whisky. He did not feel at all drunk, merely clear headed and pierced. He felt that he could drink all night and not get drunk.

Eventually they went in for dinner. He felt the room warm and stuffy but he was in a funny mood. He suddenly said, "I'm going to buy a bottle of wine," though he had never done so in his life before. She looked at him rather disapprovingly as if she didn't want to see him wasting his money so extravagantly, but she didn't say anything. In fact he felt rather quarrelsome. He laughed when the waiter obsequiously poured a little wine into his glass for him to taste it and waited for him deferentially to say if it was good enough though he knew nothing about wine. He wondered what the waiter would say if he suddenly said in a loud biblical voice, "This is rotten wine. Take it away. This is sinful wine. This is an offence against the lower classes." He felt rather giggly. Everything seemed to amuse him, the pictures on the walls, with their silly deer and hills, the French names of the foods.

"Are you going to dance later?" he asked.

"If you like," she said.

"It's not me, it's you," he said. "I don't dance. I never learned to dance. I can't do anything that requires balance." Again he found this rather funny, himself moving about the world in an unbalanced way, falling over chairs and tables, singing. He nearly burst out laughing but managed to restrain himself. The waiter was looking across at him, a serviette in his hand. Silly little man, he thought. What an extraordinary, absurd life. What servitude. He thought, if one had enough money one could go to the best hotels. But he was nearly broke and he didn't know when he would get some more. He drank his wine quickly, feeling all the same that it was not a good thing to mix wine and whisky.

"If you want to go after the meal," she said to him.

"No, we'll stay," he insisted. "We'll see what the dance is like." Something was singing at the back of his mind purely and insanely. He knew that something strange was happening to him, something irreversible, that he was being mixed like dough, but he persuaded himself that it was simply that he was drunk. Nevertheless he knew that all the contradictions in his life had come together and were laid before him as in a game lying on a table and that they were screaming with pain. He wanted to pour wine over them so that he couldn't see them any more. He hadn't often been drunk before. He wanted to make loud jokes which would annoy the waiter, but at the same time he didn't want to embarrass Ann. She was eating carefully and seriously. She belonged to the real world of people, of banal pictures, and in some way he couldn't define he himself didn't. And that was why he was drinking.

Why had she never married? It wasn't that she was ugly. In fact the more he drank the prettier she seemed to become. It wasn't that she was unsuited to the world. She was certainly more suited to it than he was. She was attractive to men; the boys back in the bar had been smiling at her. They would probably have liked to talk to her. And it wasn't as if she belonged to him though he didn't know what he could do without her. She was serene and calm. She never spoke unless she had something to say. He imagined being married to her and saw as if in a flash of nightmare the demonic face of Dixon standing at the window peering in. How could they be together as long as Dixon existed? Wherever they went Dixon would follow them, the eternal laughing enigmatic face devouring him.

"You'd better eat your meat," she said, "otherwise you'll get drunk."

"All right," he said obediently, "that's what I'm doing." He drank some more wine. He hated the dining room and the waiter, servile silly bugger. As long as one had money the world was one's oyster but without money what would happen to one? And that waiter, he knew, would have summed him up. He would know him to a T, that was part of his training. A servant of the money world, twisted internally by envy but showing a calm dignified external face. His face had the glitter that one would get from a polished silvery pan, meaningless, hard, merciless. A toady of the upper classes.

"I'd like to kick that bugger in the teeth," he said.

"Who?" said Ann looking up in a startled manner.

"That waiter," he said.

"I think," she said calmly, "I'd like Peach Melba." Her calmness was like balm to him. To be so calm always, never to suffer the storms of the mind, to have a perpetual compass . . . that would be heaven.

"I shall marry her," he thought, "no matter what happens. It's the only thing that will save me. If she will marry me," and he felt happy as if he had solved something though it was only the wine swirling around in his head.

"I think," he said, "I'll go to the lavatory."

"All right," she said.

He stumbled a little as he left the room under the gaze of the waiter and eventually found the lavatory. He stared down dully as he unzipped his fly, feeling as if he were in a hospital surrounded by white tiles. After he had finished he went to the basin and tried to be sick and while he was doing so a tall man in a bow tie came in and combed his hair peacefully in the mirror. Christ, thought Tom, Dixon again, he follows me everywhere, and he had an almost overwhelming urge to hit the man on the nose. No matter how much he tried to be sick he couldn't, but he washed his face and the cold water soothed him. He walked back down the corridor seeing ahead of him the head of the stuffed deer and went into the dining room again. He sat down to his sweet.

"Are you all right?" Ann asked him.

"Yes," he said but he was sweating and he didn't feel at all well. However, when he took some more wine he felt that if he was going to be drunk, he might as well make a good job of it.

"They usually serve the coffee in the lounge according to the waitress," said Ann. "You'd better have black coffee."

"All right," he said.

Together they went into the lounge and sat in chairs in front of the fire, which was so warm that Tom almost fell asleep.

"Are you sure you don't want to go away?" she said.

"No," he said half angrily. "No."

"All right, if that's what you want. Do you want an aspirin?"

"No. No thanks."

He drank the black coffee, when it came, gratefully, and slowly, as if it were a bomb or a mine, unfolded the bill. It came to five pounds odd and he paid it but didn't leave a tip. He was trying to remember how much money he had, but couldn't. It was very hot in the room.

"Do you want to go back to the bar?" he said.

"If you like."

They got up and walked along to the bar and found seats in a crowded part of the room. The folk singer was still playing his guitar and there was a lot of noise.

"What will you have?" he asked Ann.

"A shandy," she said, "but I don't think you should have anything."

"A shandy and a whisky," he said to the girl who, as she leaned over, showed the tops of her breasts.

Steadily his head began to fill, as if with whisky. He heard himself now and again singing. He heard himself now and again requesting the guitar player to play certain tunes. The strings of the guitar were like a woman's hair which the man was stroking. He saw the two boys smiling at Ann. Once he leaned over to Ann and said, "I love you," and she said, "I love you." Then surprisingly he found that there was a dance in a room opening off the bar. He was standing at the bar drinking while Ann danced. Now and again she would come up and talk to him but most of the time he saw her dancing gaily and happily. At first it was nice that she should be so happy. He himself stood or swayed by the bar drinking, knowing that he had very little money left. But as he watched he saw that more and more she was dancing with the fair-haired boy and that as she danced she was looking up at him and laughing, and he was filled with a desolating rage. But he remained where he was, the anger simmering in him like whisky while the accordions played, and the dancers swayed in front of him happily, forgetful of themselves, allowing their bodies to speak.

He stumbled out and found himself in the darkness pierced in flashes by the moon. There was a statue or something in front of him. He stood up and clung to it and close up he saw that it had a simpering Greek face. He stared at it for a long time thinking. Shall I go back and shout? Shall I scream? Shall I make a scene? But he didn't know if he should do that. He was overwhelmed by the hotel's air of ease and riches and happiness. He felt around in the half darkness not knowing what he was looking for. Did she really love him? Was it possible? He felt a stone in his hand and without thinking began banging it methodically in the face of the Greek statue. It was Dixon he was hitting, it was Dixon and all he stood for, the lying reason, the silly wit, the pretentiousness. He was weeping with frustration as he banged away at the face. "God damn you," he shouted over and over, but no one heard him. "God damn you to hell."

After he had disfigured the statue enough he made his staggering way down the path to the road. He didn't know where he was going and he didn't care. Sometimes he was proud of himself as he walked along, how well he could walk. Sometimes he thought that he must look ridiculous. But most of the time he concentrated on walking, putting one foot in front of the other. He decided, I can't walk into the city, it's too far away. I must get a lift. He stopped at the side of the road and waved to cars passing but none stopped. Eventually a large lorry did so and he climbed in. The lorry driver, large and looming, said :

"Had a bucket, eh?" Tom lolled back against the seat.

"Where do you want to get to?" said the lorry driver. In front of him was a half-chewed sandwich.

"Put me down in the centre," said Tom half asleep. "The centre."

"Where did you get that skinful?" said the lorry driver.

"Party," said Tom, "party," waving a hand vaguely. "Bloody party." For the life of him he couldn't sit up straight. "Bloody party," he repeated monotonously.

"If you say so," said the lorry driver humorously.

"If you say so."

Now and again Tom would wake up and say, "Bloody party" as if it were some sort of password. The lorry driver leaned forward and bit into the sandwich. You certainly got them, even at midnight. Even later. No use talking to this one, he was too far gone.

Once Tom woke up and said, "Women, know about women?"

"Women, mate?" said the lorry driver. "Are you asking me if I know about women?"

"Women?" said Tom earnestly, trying to lean forward. "Know about women? Bitches. Unreashonable bitches. Thash what."

Suddenly he began to sing, *Waly Waly*. Then abruptly fell silent.

"Unreashonable bitches. Bloody party," he repeated sullenly. "Not like men, not like us."

"You're bloody right there, mate," said the lorry driver, calmly negotiating a bend. He felt rather superior to this odd boy. Something had certainly happened to him.

"Not like ush," said Tom again managing to sit up and thrusting one finger forward like a lawyer in court.

"Utterly unlike ush. Bugger ush up. Right?"

"Dead right, mate," said the lorry driver. "Dead right."

Tom was bent on pursuing the matter to its ultimate conclusion. "Closher to earth. Children. Cavesh. Right?" His eyes squinted vaguely at the lorry driver and then he sank down again, snoring.

After some time the lorry driver said, "Well, mate, this is the city centre. Where do you want to get off?"

"Anywhere," said Tom with an effort. "Anywhere, old mate. Anywhere at all."

Eventually without quite knowing how, he found himself on the street and recognised the railway station. He made his way unsteadily inside and lay down on a bench and went to sleep.

22

H E D I D N ' T W A K E up till eight o'clock in the morning and at first he didn't know where he was. He didn't feel at all cold though it was chilly. His shoes, he noticed, had blades of wet grass on them and the bottoms of his trousers were damp. Ahead of him he could see a train gently puffing smoke. He had an unaccountable impulse to climb into a carriage without bothering to find out where the train was going. The train, puffing smoke and rocking slightly on the rails in preparation for departure, seemed to be a symbol for some motion in himself. He did not feel at all despairing, rather he felt fresh as if a fever had worked itself out in him. The morning seemed large and clear though chilly and the continual movement of people passing him and the imminent departure of the train interested him. He felt as if something were beginning in him, though he couldn't tell what it was, as if he had come to some unknown decision in his sleep. Women shushing their children, men reading the morning papers, boys drinking orangeade while waiting for their parents to buy tickets, they were all part of the real world. The bench on which he was sitting, whose green paint was flaking in places, was also part of it.

For some odd reason he had a fantasy about the Prodigal Son which was in some way connected with the bench and the events of the previous night. He imagined the Prodigal Son leaving his home on a bristly autumn morning while his mother waved to him. He was carrying a bag which contained all his worldly goods, he was setting off into the world.

There was dew on the thorns, the brown autumn earth was rich and heavy, he walked along in the sharp air humming to himself. He climbed on to a bus which would take him to another country. The bus made its way along between avenues of trees with cold red berries on them. He got off the bus after a long while and began to look for work.

He could not find any and eventually ended up sitting on a bench just like the bench he himself was sitting on. Time passed and it was Christmas, and people were walking past with their parcels clutched in their hands. He saw the warm squares of windows. He himself sat day after day on the bench looking down at his windowed boots. His body was covered by a newspaper so that he looked like a collage by Picasso. His face was bristly. He remembered farms and pigs, he remembered sleeping out, he saw prostitutes passing by on their high heels, priced and unattainable. The whole world was a shop and he had his nose up against the pane but he couldn't buy anything.

Suddenly Tom got up both in his imagined role of Prodigal Son and as himself. He knew that there was somewhere he must get to. As he walked along he imagined himself going home to his father and brother. When he got off the bus he would see his brother working in the fields with the same rusty scythe that he had always used. He was composing in his mind his new role of humility, that of the penitent returned. He was repeating the words of his speech over and over. There was a party and frail balloons floating in the sky, there were accordions playing. He went to his room which contained a rocking horse and his books and other toys, still lying there undisturbed, the disorderly data of the preconscious. He stood in front of the mirror and practised his speech. He would go to his father and say, "I have come home. I am the Penitent. Call me the Prodigal Son." And he knew that his father would listen to him though perhaps not his brother. He would settle on the farm, ordinary, common, accepting what the day brought, no longer setting out for unattainable countries, even the ones closest to home.

As he walked along immersed in his story he smelt the odour of bacon and eggs and realised that he was hungry. He went into the cafe and ordered some breakfast knowing that he had only ten pounds or so left. But he did not feel worried because deep down he had come to a decision though as yet he didn't know what it was. He ate his bacon and eggs quickly and when he had finished walked out again. He knew that if he let himself go he would be taken to where he ought to be. All he had to do was to let his body work. He did not feel at all frightened. So he let himself walk and as he walked he recognised where he was going. He recognised a part of the city which he had not visited for a long time. He passed a large prison with high grey walls and a school with dull brown walls. It was a part of his past, disorderly and dirty, certainly not the White City of elitism and culture.

Once a beggar came up to him and asked him for a few pence, pulling at his cap and calling him Sir. He didn't give him anything because he needed all the money he had. Nor did he feel any sense of guilt. He was quite rigorous about his refusal and quite realistic. He knew that the man was trying to con him, and he didn't feel any anger but he wasn't going to give away his money uselessly. It was as if he were awakening from a long dream or sickness and in the light of reality he saw the world as it really was, not condemnable but inevitable. He passed a bookshop but did not stop at it. He was impatient to gather together what he had been, what he was.

Once he stopped and looked for a long time at a man who

was burning an old railing away with an acetylene torch. The flame hovered bluely in the blue chill of the day. The man who was wearing a yellow helmet was whistling gaily as he concentrated on his work. What he was doing was burning away an old railing and that was good enough for him, it was his job, it was what he was trained to do, he was absorbed in his work. He did not look at all self-conscious while Tom stood staring at him and at his torch as it ate away the old rusty brown railings, the blue flame hissing and burning powerfully.

Tom moved on through the maze of streets. He remembered this place very well. He had often passed it on the way to the cinema which was called the Scala. It was old and cramped, contorted, crowded with slums. There used to be a lot of drunks wandering about here, he remembered. As early as this in the morning, however, there weren't many people about. There was an air of emptiness about the place, as if it had exhausted itself, there were advertisements on the walls, one in particular which said forlornly, FIGHT HEATH. He walked steadily on, seeing in the distance and to his right great cranes high up in the sky, tall factory chimneys belching out smoke.

It was after nine o'clock when he stopped outside the school. There was the same stony playground, the same long sad windows. At the back, he knew, were the streaming privies with the nicknames of pupils and assorted obscenities scrawled on the walls. The bicycle shed was still there with bicycles racked in it. Did he really want to go in there? Was this where his feet had led him? For a long time he hovered, now he would go in, now he wouldn't. Once he walked on for a few yards but then retraced his steps. It wasn't that he had liked the place, rather he had disliked it. It wasn't even that he expected to find any revelation here.

Even now he could smell damp clothes drying on radiators, urine in boys' browned lavatories. But it was as if some secret voice were telling him that he must go in, that there was a solution hidden here somewhere, though he couldn't imagine what solution he was looking for; that there was some obligation on him to make some discovery which would be important to him. Hesitantly he pushed open the gate and entered.

When he opened the main door he found himself in the hall and there by astonishing chance met his old English teacher Richardson. He stood there for a moment staring at him, in his long coat, staggered by the conflicting feelings that swirled about in him. Richardson had changed and yet was still the same. He had grown older and dimmer, but he still bore about with him an air of hauteur. He seemed larger, more florid, coarser, lacking in definition, and yet at the same time he still seemed to convey the idea that one must consider him exceptional. He was carrying some books in his arms and was clearly going to his room with them. He looked at Tom who was standing hesitantly in the hall.

"Are you looking for someone?" he asked. And then as he recognised him he seemed to flush and lose his poise.

"Spence," said Tom automatically. "You printed some of my stuff in the school magazine some years ago."

"Of course," said Richardson. "That coat ... for the moment ..." He seemed confused and dithery and gestured vaguely, forgetting that he had books in his arms, so that he nearly dropped them.

"Changed days? What are you doing now?" His voice had assumed a slightly mocking sardonic quality as if he were practising a tone he had forgotten.

"Nothing much, I'm afraid."

"I see, I see." Richardson seemed to hover as if he didn't

quite know what to say and then added, "And what do you think of the old place, eh? Still recognisable, I suppose?"

"Just the same," said Tom. He was filled with a vast unease as he regarded this figure whom he had once adored, who was still, however, jauntily wearing a bow tie, still striving to be witty.

"Still the same Miltonic pillars, eh? The same cloisters? And were you just passing?" he asked ironically.

"That's right," said Tom, "just passing."

"Good, good," Richardson said heartily. "Good to see pupils. One of them came to see me the other day. He's working on physics. A thesis. Naturally I couldn't make out what he was talking about. He seemed very prosperous and eager. These poems of yours, have you continued with them?"

"Not much."

"They were very gloomy I remember. Strange how adolescents write such doom-filled poems. Are your poems still gloomy or doomy?"

"I don't write many now."

"I see, I see."

Unspoken thoughts hung between them. Tom was thinking how hollow Richardson's words sounded. Had he always been like this really? If Tom had been old enough, would he have sensed their hollowness even then? But surely they hadn't been hollow in those days? Surely not. Richardson shifted his books awkwardly. There seemed to be a draught in the hall rippling the old worn linoleum.

"Well," said Richardson at last, "must feed the maws. Glad to have seen you. I'd shake hands but I can't, you see, with these books. You should carry on with your writing. It's always something to do. I didn't recognise you at first. It must be the clothes. That's what it must be. Well, cheerio."

Tom stood there for a moment staring after him, then left the hall and went outside. He was thinking how different the school was from Ann's, how dead and dull, how lifeless, how infinitely dreary; but something else was troubling him as he walked along. At the back of his mind a clue was niggling, yet he couldn't make out what the clue was or what puzzle it would serve to unlock. But at the same time he did feel like a detective trying to piece together a crime from scattered errors, flashes of recognition.

He knew it was something to do with Richardson and he tried to remember what he could about him. Richardson's were quite simply the only classes he had liked. In those days Richardson was different from what he had evidently now become. He had been enthusiastic and eager, he had about him an air of hauteur and wit. It wasn't a cold wit, it was rather a spontaneous wit that welled up from a surplusage of life. He would enter a class as if bearing gifts, as if he were some emissary sent to make the school less dull, more vibrant. He had noticed Tom's essays and stories, he had drawn attention to them, sometimes he had read them to the class. At a time when Tom felt he was no good at anything Richardson had helped him to survive. He had wanted to be like Richardson, a pure flame of the mind, of himself alone.

Richardson was completely unpredictable and worked to no system except his own, as if he believed that his own mind and its workings, freed of any curriculum, was bound to be of interest to others. Sometimes he would enter during a period scheduled for some dreary author and say, "We won't do that today. I've just been reading a book on surnames." Then he would go round the class and find out the surnames and they would spend a happy period trying to disentangle their meanings. That had been a particularly hilarious period, and Jean as usual had been entranced with admiration.

Jean? who was Jean? He stopped, wondering. Why had Jean come into his mind now? She seemed to float, pale-faced, up to his mind, and yet he couldn't remember her surname. She always wore a white blouse or at least that was the impression he had, if he was thinking of the right girl. He could see her tight bum which had often attracted him but he couldn't remember her full name. He simply had the impression of Richardson lecturing—for that was what he did—emitting intellectual sparkles, self-glorying, humorous, while Jean sat in the next seat to his own, her face cradled in her hands, openly adoring.

He tried to visualise the blackboard while Richardson scrawled across it. Nothing was ever written systematically. The blackboard was a disordered mess of fragments of lessons on surnames, Browning (whom he liked) and snatches of ideas from scientific books. Tom felt that the surnames were important. Spence. A spence of spirit in a waste of shame. Sir Somebody Spens. What was the man's first name? Surely it wasn't Tom. Sir Thomas Spens. It didn't sound right.

Jean what? It was impossible, he couldn't get the name right. It was all very puzzling and almost painful as he made the effort of remembering. What did he know even about Richardson? Nothing much. He had been animated and alert and interesting but Tom didn't know anything about his background. He didn't even know whether he belonged to the city. And did Jean belong to the city? He couldn't remember that either. And there must be a reason for that since he could remember quite vividly her freckled face, white blouse and trim bum. He could see her entering the room late while the class were working on a lesson. She always seemed to be late, it must have been something to do with a bus, in which case she might not have come from the city at all. It was during the time of puberty that he had felt that

166

terrible lust for her, so she must have been in the same class as him for perhaps two or three years.

Why in fact had he visited the school at all when it was disturbing him so much? But no matter how hard he tried to concentrate he could hear only the quick jesting voice of Richardson and see Jean with her face cradled in her hands which rested on the desk. He couldn't even remember much that Richardson had actually said. It had been more a matter of atmosphere, of airy nothings, of transitory witticisms.

Though he could remember nothing much about Jean he felt that he was on the trail of something that was important to him. Richardson's blond hair was also important, though he couldn't think why. It was painful to try and use his memory as intensely as that, as if there was a block some- where. Perhaps he didn't want to remember, perhaps that was it. Of course Richardson's hair wasn't so blond now, in fact he seemed to have very little hair at all. Also he hadn't spoken so brightly, so gaily. Perhaps he had settled down like fizzy lemonade, become flat. And yet he had admired Richardson so much, he had thought of him as a free spirit, *sui generis*. It was a pure mind at play, it was like water sparkling in sunlight. He had seemed to him so unlike his father. He stopped as if he had stepped on a mine. Why his father? Richardson wasn't remotely like his father. Not physically at any rate. Was it perhaps that he had thought that Richardson was making real use of his books while his father was scribbling his ridiculous jejune notes? Was that it? It might easily have been that.

There was Richardson transmitting his knowledge, forming minds, gaining glory from the word and there was his father, sheltering in his shed, running away, a dreamer. Could that be it? Richardson my father ... RICHARDSON MY FATHER. The three words seemed to be a detonator, he could feel the small tremors and the explosions but they didn't mean anything to him. After all Richardson hadn't been all that much older than him, not that much. He hadn't been old at all, why think of him as of a father? Surely that was nonsense. Was there something else then? His father had simply read books, had written little notes about their plots, but he had been really an ignorant man. But why had he and the other pupils thought of Richardson as different from the other teachers? He had spoken with authority. Where had he come from? Who was he? Tom stopped on the pavement and stared restlessly about him. He hardly recognised where he was. Something about Richardson, about his father perhaps . . .

And these poems he had written for the school magazine. Could he remember them, any of them? One of them had been entitled "Love". Something about, "Betrayal comes down in clouds of gold . . ."

Now what the devil did that mean? The usual sordid unhappy schoolboyish image? Perhaps. Perhaps that was all it was. But his mind was simmering. He knew it was close to something important, some boiling point, but he couldn't focus on it. The best thing would be to leave it. The puzzle might open itself out voluntarily. He stared up and found that his feet had brought him on to his own house.

23

OR RATHER TO his father's and mother's house. It was strange to be looking at it. To think that he had lived there, that he had slept there. It was a most peculiar sensation like standing in the street staring up at himself. But the curtains on the living room windows were different. In the old days they had been red, now they were green. That made him uneasy, for his mother had disliked green. "It's a colour for Catholics," she used to say. The gate too had been painted green. It was all very odd. It made him feel slightly at the edge of the world.

He went to the door and rang the bell which also was a different one. It made a chiming, falling sound when he pressed it. Just after he had rung the bell he saw that the name on the door wasn't Spence at all, it was Docherty. He stood there shaken, for he had expected that his mother would still be there. What had happened to her? A youngish plump woman with slightly deranged black hair stood looking at him. She looked as if she had just got out of bed, there was an aura of sleepy warmth about her.

He said, "I'm sorry. I seem to have made a mistake. I used to live here. I didn't realise. I've been away . . ."

"I beg your pardon?" she said smoothing her hair. He noticed that she spoke in a slightly affected voice.

He repeated what he had said.

"Oh," she said at last, intelligence dawning in her eyes. "I suppose your name must be Spence. We heard about you."

He felt suddenly angry that she should know about him,

that they had been gossiping about him, that his name had been bandied about without his knowledge.

"If you would care to come in," she said. "I'm sorry. I've just got up. I'll make you a cup of tea." He hesitated and then followed her. The hall was utterly different. The wallpaper, once dark brown, was now a bright yellow. There was a hallstand and a large oval mirror above it. He had the impression that the whole house was brighter, alive with colour. He was baffled and at odds with himself.

"I don't suppose you'll recognise the place," she said. And he didn't. Furniture seemed to be in different places and was of a different kind, lighter, sunnier. As he walked along the lobby he thought for a frantic moment that even his own bedroom had disappeared. But certainly the door was still there though it was painted in a light grey colour. He could hear a child crying somewhere. The whole place hurt him. It was too brash, too colourful.

"My husband's just gone off to work," she said. "He's in insurance. You can have a look at the rooms if you like while I make a cup of tea," she said comfortably. She seemed to have no fear of him and to have accepted his story, and this angered him slightly. It was as if she didn't think much of him, as if she could afford to ignore him.

He went to his own bedroom and looked inside. That place too he couldn't recognise. The red armchair was gone and in its place was a smooth leather-covered contraption all in black. There were some bright paintings on the walls, one showing what appeared to be an Italian scene. There was a picture of the Virgin Mary holding a greenish Jesus in her arms. There were no books at all in the room, only a record player in the corner. The counterpane on the bed was a bright yellow : his own had been blue.

He felt shattered as if some demon had come in the night

and changed his world around. When he heard her busy with a kettle in the kitchenette he thought for a moment it was his mother and he almost shouted automatically in an angry preoccupied voice that he wouldn't be long. For a moment he felt so tired that he nearly lay down on the bed in order to sleep.

When he went out again she was sitting in the living room with cups of tea on a tray. The living room too had been changed. There was a large electric fire, the carpet was a pale green (instead of flowery), there were more pictures on the walls (mostly of landscapes) and there was a vase on the shining table with paper flowers in it.

"You'll find a big difference," she said. She had combed her hair and looked fresher. He didn't look on her as a person at all, he regarded her as a stranger who would give him information.

She offered him the tea. She had already put sugar in it and it was very sweet.

"We moved in four months ago," she said. "Charles was working very hard on it but it's all right now. Not that it wasn't in good condition," she added hastily.

"No," Tom said automatically, sipping his tea.

"I'm afraid," she said looking at him rather sharply, "your mother's no longer here." He thought at first that she was saying that his mother had moved somewhere else, but realised by the way that she took her eyes from him and looked down at the floor that his mother had died.

"But the neighbours could tell you more," she added. "The Robertsons and Thomsons are still here. They'll be able to tell you."

Suddenly he said, as if it was the most important thing of all, "What happened to the shed?"

"I beg your pardon?"

"The shed in the garden. Is it still there? At the back?"

"Oh, the shed," she said. "I couldn't think for a moment. Yes, the shed's still there. Charles keeps his tools there. He makes things, you know. Furniture. Shelves. Things like that. He spends a lot of his time there. He works in insurance you know. But he likes working with his hands. Would you like to see it?"

"What?"

"The shed. Would you like to see it?"

"No, no, it's all right. I don't want to see it."

"You could if you wanted to. I know what it must be like for you. I'm very sorry. Would you like some more tea?"

"No thanks. Thank you very much. It was very good of you to ask me in."

"Not at all. You must find this place very strange."

"Yes, I do. I do rather."

"I'm sure. Would you like a biscuit?"

"No thanks. I'll have to be going."

"Yes of course. If you want to be going."

Tom could almost hear echoing through the house his mother's stormy voice. He himself was running in from somewhere panting, sweating. She was telling him that he was late as usual for his dinner.

He got up feeling slightly dizzy, his eyes wet. The curtains were billowing greenly in a fresh breeze, the incomprehensible curtains. Beyond the window he could see the blue sky with the nameless clouds passing across it. How much of pain there was in the world. How much one had to learn and suffer. To see one's house being transformed was like changing one's nature.

"I'll go next door," he said. "I'll ask the Robertsons. It was kind of you to give me the tea."

"Not at all," she said again. "I'm only sorry I had to give

you such bad news." He felt ill and unshaven and had another fantasy of himself sitting up in his bed in his own old room as the grandmother while the wolf entered, tall and elegant and suave. The wolf had the face of Dixon, witty and debonair.

She saw him to the door and he hesitated a moment before going up to the Robertsons' house. At the back of his own old home he could see the shed. It also had been painted green. The door was open and he could see the tools quite clearly. Well perhaps it was more suitable for tools anyway. And why not? That was what people usually kept in sheds.

As he walked up to the Robertsons' house a picture of Ann came into his mind and he gritted his teeth lest he should scream. She was lying down among trees, legs spread apart, and above her was the head of a man with blond hair. Suddenly she rose and began to limp away crying to him for help but he did not answer. He stopped at the gate, gazing into space, his face working convulsively.

Mrs Robertson on her way to do her shopping, scarfed and carrying a purse, was about to push him aside when she stopped, recognising him.

"Tom Spence," she said loudly, as if she had made a great discovery. "Tom Spence. What are you doing here?"

He looked at her, vaguely struggling out of his dream, and muttered, "I'm sorry, I . . ."

"You don't look well, boy. Would you like to come in for a moment? I expect you've been told about your mother. Is that it?"

"Yes," he said, "I . . ."

"Come inside. The shopping will stay till later."

But even as she brought him in she was thinking what she would have to tell her friends later on. "Betty's son, that one she said was going to be a bank manager, he came to the house this morning. Looked like a ghost too."

A large fat man who nodded to him but did not speak and thereafter retired behind a large newspaper was sitting in a chair beside the fire in the living room.

"I'll make you a cup of tea," said Mrs Robertson briskly. "I won't be long. Not a jiffy. You wait there."

Tom stared dully at the large mirror above the mantelpiece, the china cats, the flickering of the fire.

Eventually Mrs Robertson came in with the tea and some cakes which she laid down on a small table in front of him. He drank some of the tea but did not eat any of the cakes.

"You know of course that your mother passed away," said Mrs Robertson, looking at him keenly. "Not very long ago. They tried to find you but they couldn't. There was a notice in the paper."

"I don't read the papers," he said.

"I see," she said disapprovingly as if this confirmed her worst forebodings. "Anyway she had a good end." Might as well tell him that though she had been going about with that man, that unsuitable working class fellow. "Let's see now," she said. "It's some years since you left home, isn't it? I remember it very well. You didn't think I saw you, did you? You left with your books. I remember it very well. It was on a summer's morning. Must have been in your last term at school. That's right, isn't it?" A shudder shook him again, chill and menacing. "I remember it was a very fine summer's morning. The blinds were still down on your house. I didn't know you were leaving home of course, though I thought it was funny. You looked very secretive."

"What did my mother die of?" he asked.

"She was ill. Pneumonia I think. She didn't suffer much.

The neighbours were good to her but in the end they had to take her to the hospital."

So she was lying in hospital while he was working on his book, while he was perhaps at that party. No, that couldn't be, that other woman had said four months ago. Yet he didn't care for her very much. Why therefore did he feel so sad? He thought of her desperate attempt to make something of both her husband and himself, and of the wedding he had seen. She too had once been young and perhaps beautiful. Later she had become embittered and nagging. When he was a child she would buy him presents. He remembered a small cart and a small white horse which he would trundle across the floor, pulling at the golden harness.

"Where is she buried?" he said.

"In Larkhill Cemetery," she said. "Your aunt put up a stone I believe. You'll find it easily enough."

Miles and miles of headstones, how could he find it easily enough?

"When she was in hospital she sold the house, so I've heard. You should go and see the lawyer." He knew the lawyer's name but he didn't know whether he would go. She liked having a lawyer, she would say things like, "My lawyer told me that I should sell the house and buy another one." Now she was dead; she must have known that she would never leave the hospital. She and his father had been married when they were quite young. He had started in the bank and together at dinner time they must have walked down the street hand in hand, years ago. She would have predicted a great future for him then, and perhaps he did for himself too. But the future hadn't happened. She had been quite an ordinary girl, the kind who goes to dances and thinks of having children. She had two sisters who never came to visit and she hadn't encouraged her mother and father to come to the house. Perhaps she was ashamed of them.

He stood up suddenly, his eyes smarting. "I'll go and see the lawyer," he said though he had no intention of doing so. "And I'll go to the cemetery."

"Yes, you do that," said Mrs Robertson. "You do that." She thought he looked sickly and not very well dressed but it wasn't her business. Serve him right in a way for going away like that and causing his mother heartbreak. After all mothers were mothers, they shouldn't be treated like that. She was glad to see him go, he looked too broken and over-dignified. She had seen that kind of dignity before in those men who had little else left. She looked thankfully around her room and at her husband who was still hidden behind his newspaper.

Tom didn't think he would go to the lawyer after all, it would be too complicated. And in any case he didn't want the money from the house even if it had been left him. Perhaps it had been left to the little man, whoever he was. And as he thought about that he realised that he wanted to see the little man to see what he was like. So he returned and asked Mrs Robertson and she looked at him oddly as if she hadn't realised that he hadn't known, but she gave him the address and he went there as the cold morning blossomed about the tenements and the ugly streets.

It was funny how he had found out about the little man. It was in fact Crawford who had told him, for Crawford kept up his connection with the place from which he had come, perhaps because he had read somewhere that one of the great dangers for the academic was contempt for his origins, a schizophrenia of the spirit. One night he had told Tom that he was making a great mistake in cutting himself off from his roots. "A writer can't do without his roots," he had said. "No writer has ever written well when he has cut himself off from his roots." And it was then that he had let the information slip out. And it was only another reason then why Tom felt that he couldn't go back. But now he desperately wanted to see the little man, he wanted to talk to him, since there was no one else to talk to.

But as he walked along there was eating at him Mrs Robertson's remark about his departure on that summer morning "in his last term". It was these words which disturbed him for some particular reason and which made him feel so chilly. Not simply the fact that it had been a summer's morning but that it had been his last term. Why had he left? He stopped in the middle of the road and swayed, just about to cross. A car swished past him and he heard a distant shout and realised what had almost happened. He ran quickly away from any trouble that might have ensued. The name Richardson was beating about in his head. At first he had confused it with Robertson but he knew that the name he was looking for was really Richardson. And he knew it had something to do with a girl, not Ann, not Sheila, but Jean. She had been trim and attractive, not very clever, but reasonably bright. But he couldn't remember whether they had meant anything to each other.

So lost was he in his thoughts that he passed the address which had been given to him and came back slowly again, searching the numbers till eventually he found the right one, 42. 43 Somerville Street.

The name, he had been told disapprovingly by Mrs Robertson, was Niven. On the other hand Fred Niven might not be at home. After all it was after ten o'clock, nearly eleven, and if he was working he would be at work. Perhaps Tom's mother had left the money from the house to this

Fred Niven. Tom found it strange to be climbing this dark staircase to meet a complete stranger who had apparently been something to his mother. The name was on a nameplate at the very top: the stair had spiralled round a dark, deep well which had made Tom slightly dizzy. When he reached the door he pressed the yellow bell and waited. For a while there was silence and then some scramblings and mutterings. After what seemed a long time a small bald man with a wrinkled brow came to the door, rubbing his eyes. He was wearing a blue shirt but no jacket and his trousers seemed to be held up by what looked like a pyjama cord. He looked vaguely at Tom as if he thought he might be the rent or the electricity man. For a long moment they looked at each other.

"My name is Tom Spence," said Tom.

Niven stared at him uncomprehendingly. It occurred to Tom that he might be recovering from a hangover. "My mother ..." he began.

Light dawned in the washed blue eyes, secretive and hostile and defensive.

"Come in, come in," said Niven and Tom walked into the half darkness. The curtains of the kitchen were still drawn and he had an impression of full ashtrays and bottles lying on the floor beside a phantom armchair islanded in the half light.

Niven pulled the curtains aside and revealed what Tom had half seen, an armchair covered with a blue cloth, empty beer bottles on the floor, a sink full of dishes.

"I havena been to work for a few days," said Niven dusting off a chair for Tom to sit on. "Ever since ... It's not a few days. It's weeks," he added. "Would ye like a beer?" he asked almost slyly, "or a nip?"

"No thanks," said Tom, "not just now. It's too early."

"Aye it's that, it's early. The day's so long," said Niven, "ever since." His voice strengthened. "We met, your mother and me, at a social. We had a drink or two, nothing much, mind you, your mother was a respectable woman, being married to a bank manager an' all. We were lonely people, ye see. We used to go to the park now and again and sit and watch the ducks. Sometimes we'd go to the flicks. She'd tell me about you and how well you were doing. We were company for each other, understand? Mind you, there was gossip, but we didna mind. We had no one else, see? Afore I met her I had my pigeons but I gave them up. Would you like a cup of tea then?"

"No thanks, I just had one," said Tom.

"Your mother was a strange woman. She wanted me to get a business o' my ain but I had nae money. She'd show me your father's books, a' thae books he'd read. She used to cook for me. I laid off the drink when I knew her. Not a drop touched my lips hardly. She was too good for me, I knew that. She was a kind woman, she used to wash my clothes. Sometimes I'd go to her house and she'd come to mine, but I never married her. It was companionship, see? Sometimes she'd sit there in that chair and say that she'd not done very well for you, but that she'd tried her best. She used to say that, 'I tried my best but I didn't understand them.' That's what she used to say. And I used to comfort her. Not that I could give her much o' that. A few weeks back she complained of a bad cold but she wouldn't go to bed and then she got the pneumonia. And they took her to hospital. I used to go along with grapes and she would lie there and not say anything. One night a man came to my door and told me she had died. And I took to the drink again, that's what I did." Tom suddenly realised that the man was crying and he had never seen a man crying before.

"It's all right," he found himself saying, "it's all right. It wasn't your fault. It was my fault. I shouldn't have left her."

After a while, after wiping his eyes with a large soiled handkerchief, Niven continued : "Mind you, she had a temper too. And she wanted to improve me, as she called it, but it was too late. Some nights we quarrelled but we always went back to each other, since there was no one else."

"I understand," said Tom. He felt sluices inside him opening as if at last he was in touch with some reality that he actually felt and did not simply know about. His book and his preoccupations seemed very far away, as if they belonged to a dream world, except that at the centre there was Ann. He had another vision which seemed to imprint itself on the grimy wall. There was a fire and a smiling fair-haired man and a limping girl. The man was saying to him, "You shouldn't have done that, you know." He, Tom, had smashed a bottle of wine in the limping girl's hand. He ran away as the man raised his stick. He was running through a desert but as he looked behind him he saw the two of them releasing hawks which followed him. He knew that wherever he went the two of them would be waiting for him. And sure enough they were. He found himself back at the fire, the smiling man raising a stick, the limping girl holding a rose which turned into the head of a snake swaying to no music. He began to sweat as if he had found himself in the middle of a nightmare in the daytime.

Niven was staring dully down at the floor. He was saying, "At first I couldna do anything. I couldna move. I didna want to leave the house. I didna believe it. I didna believe I wouldna see her again. So I took up the drinking again. I gave up ma work."

"You should go back," said Tom.

"What do you know about it?" said Niven aggressively. "Eh? What do you know about it? You're just a child. You left her when she needed you. She used to say that you had done well for yourself but she was lying, I can see that. You havena, have ye?" He seemed to take an unholy joy in knowing that Tom was almost as badly off as himself.

"That's true," said Tom, "she used to say things like that."

"You're right, she said," said Niven. "She was a good woman. She was a strong woman. We all let her down, that's what we did. We let her down. She was looking for someone strong but we werena strong, were we?"

"No," said Tom, "you're right, we weren't."

"What did you come here for?" said Niven again aggressively. "Were you looking for money? Did ye want to find out about the house? I didna want her money. I'd 'a done wi'oot her money."

"I know that," said Tom.

"Do you, eh? I don't know what happened to her house. Some other people are in it now. I couldn't care less about the house." He took another bottle of beer and bit the top off with a savage gesture. "You didna help her much, did you?"

Tom got to his feet. There was nothing more for him to see there. The pattern was a usual one. He himself would have to escape the pattern to know. He would have to get back, but there was something he needed to know. Richardson. Richardson. Who was Richardson? Richard. Dick. Richard, Dick. Something there if he could only get hold of it. Richardson.

Dixon.

He stood swaying in the middle of the floor while the

small man raged at him. Was that it then? Was that who Dixon had been all the while? Richardson? Yet when he looked at them both they seemed to be the same, suave, witty, knowledgeable. So why had he made Dixon the hero of the book? He had often wondered where the idea of the story had come from. Richardson too had been clever and witty and bright. Richardson had been his god when he was in school. Now Dixon was collapsing in his mind and he couldn't continue with his book. Why was that? The White City? The City of Culture, the school perhaps. Was that what it was? He felt he had grasped an essential part of the puzzle but not the whole of it. There was some part he still had to find, to grasp. And all the while Niven was shouting at him like a crazy man.

"You left her didn't you? You left her alone. You didna care. Get out. GET OUT." Tom thought he might soon come at him with a bottle. There were flecks of spittle on his mouth and he looked like a crazy man. He backed away from him, opened and shut the door and walked down the stairs. He wasn't going to run, that was for sure, but he didn't want any trouble. The stair spiralled downwards and on his side was always that deep dark well. To think that his mother had once visited that place because of her loneliness. He hadn't thought about that. He should have thought about it. She couldn't write to pass some of the time so what must her life have been? Perhaps she had started to think, perhaps she had changed, but by then it was too late. No one would care whether she had changed or not, whether she had learned. And yet perhaps she had learned to see, but there was no way of making amends. For there was no one to make amends to. Perhaps that little man had seen the best of her, perhaps she had become kindly and warm at the end. And then she had learned to accept her death. She had lain down under it for there was nowhere else to go. Perhaps he himself shouldn't have run away on that summer's morning which he couldn't clearly recollect since something in him, some obstacle, was preventing him from doing so. What was that obstacle? Why couldn't he remember? Had it occurred after some particular experience? Was that it?

He found his feet taking him steadily towards the cemetery. Without thinking he entered a flower shop. "I should like," he heard himself saying, "some flowers to put on a grave. In a vase or something." He had a vague memory of seeing some flowers in vases at cemeteries, inside marble bowls. He got the flowers and the vase and continued on his way.

As he walked along he knew that he was now finished permanently with Dixon. He knew that Dixon was a part of him which he must get rid of or die. All these books had been dreams, all these libraries had been an escape from the world. His father had used them to escape and now Richardson had done the same. For look what he had turned into, a "wee man" cracking "wee jokes". It was all a con, that spiritual aesthetic thing. There was no answer to be found in that direction. The answers were to be found in the world around when one surrendered to that world. One could only live, the questions were irrelevant since a reason for living could never be found. In all the philosophical books that had ever been written where could one find a single new *fact*, apart from interpretations of facts that had always been known, that lay around one like the rubble of the city? He had been frightened of being with other people, of touching them, of being interested in their concerns. He had been frightened even of Ann, and his jealousy was not a romantic glamour but the fear of dispossession, of solitude.

Was that not what life was about, to find at least one person one could trust, whom one could touch lightly on the shoulder as being near and true, as the companion in the terrible flux? What else was there? What else?

24

I T W A S A large cemetery, larger than any he had ever been to. The last one he had visited was while he was working on the roads. It had been very quiet, down by a loch, and he had gone and sat in it one day while eating his sandwiches. It was a very old cemetery with graves dating back to the seventeenth century. As he sat there in the sunny air, with butterflies darting about, a large rabbit had run past him, wobbling fatly. There were strong scents in the air, the noise of the water lapping on the shore mingled with the humming of bees, and once a lark rose straight up, singing. There was also, he remembered, a freshly made grave with a spade inside it, and a jacket.

But this one was different, this one was more impersonal. He supposed that like everything else even cemeteries had their different characters. It was kept neat enough and the avenues between the headstones were like streets, but it was impersonal. He had a fantasy of knocking on the large stone doors and receiving no answer in this city cemetery. He walked down each street looking for his mother's name but he couldn't see it. He would simply have to walk for a long time till he found it, that was all, for there was no one to tell him where it was. As he walked he carried the vase with its flowers, and studied the wreaths by the tombstones. Some of the flowers were lying loose, some were in vases, and now and again he would see a stone shaped like a Bible, open at a page on which the name and dates of the dead were carved. After a while he began to grow used to being in the graveyard, as if it were quite an ordinary place to be walking in. He imagined it in different seasons of the year; in the winter the wind howling about the headstones, in the spring the flowers coming up, in the late autumn the rain falling steadily and dripping from the stone.

Once to his astonishment he saw a man sitting against one of the headstones reading a comic. It was almost like a hallucination, but the man looked up and said good morning to him, and then went back to reading again. He was wearing blue dungarees and smoking a cigarette. Tom walked on, studying the gravestones. Some were as polished as mirrors so that he could almost see his own reflection in their glittering surfaces, some were old and cheap. The dead too had their orders and ranks, their poverties and riches, funny how he hadn't thought of that before. He had had some idea that when people were dead they entered an equal kingdom, but that was not the case. Even the act of burial was an economic act and those who could afford bigger and better tombstones set them up, to show that even in death they were richer than the others.

The society of the dead—and his mother inhabited it now. What was happening to her? Her bones were rotting away under there, no matter what flowers he placed above them. But bringing the flowers was a gesture of reconciliation, he sensed that. He was not exactly asking for forgiveness, he was simply entering that world which the dead were part of, and that too was a real world, the real world of death, like the world of birth and marriage. He was involved in an act of commitment. He wanted to be in that world, which was the world of everyone, which was also the world of the dead.

Once he stood resting his arm on a tombstone quite casually and found that he was completely at ease. There was a slight breeze and a blue chilly sky but it was not different from the usual sky. Those dead people hadn't changed, they weren't monsters, they had merely succumbed to what he himself would succumb to. He almost felt happy, or if not happy at least contented. And eventually he found her grave.

There was a headstone and on the headstone was written:

<blockquote>
Elizabeth Spence
dearly beloved wife
of
James Spence
1910–1970
Dead but not forgotten
</blockquote>

He stared at the stone for a long time. It was quite a nice stone, prosperous and shining, of a reddish colour. He didn't know what he was thinking. He wished that he had been there when she had died but otherwise he felt that she had gone forever and that there was nothing anyone could do about it. He couldn't summon up any hypocritical tears but he arranged the flowers and the vase and felt that the act of doing so was important. It meant that he hadn't utterly left her alone, though he didn't think of himself and her as belonging to a chain of generations. He didn't have that kind of feeling, though he knew that many people had it. Some people were very conscious of their ancestry and thought of themselves as coming at a certain point on a chain, as being significant links. He had never had that feeling.

As he rose from the gravestone he knew that he would come back now and again. All this symbolism was important. It might not be important to Dixon but it was to him. Anything that had lasted for a long time, that had been continued by thousands and millions of people, was not to be despised. That was where Dixon was wrong. The ironical laughter of someone like Dixon was not in the long run important; what was important was the ceremonies and sufferings and beliefs of the ordinary people. It was they, who never read a word that Dixon wrote, who passed final judgment on everything. It was they who spat out what was not healthy.

He got up and made his way to the gate, and as he did so his mind began to wander. He thought of Macdonald who had been working with him on the roads, a large ginger-haired fellow with high cheekbones like a gipsy's who had told him that he had sexual intercourse with a girl in a cemetery at night on a flat gravestone. "The best I ever had, boy," he had said. He had met the girl at a dance and had taken her into the cemetery at one in the morning. "There was this moon," he had said, "shining all over the names." And he had had her there. Though at first she had been frightened and superstitious but later had become passionate.

And it was then that Tom remembered it all clearly. It all flooded back to him so that he stood astonished in the middle of the cemetery. No, he hadn't known Jean very well, he hadn't been going out with her. She hadn't been a romantic date, she had just been a girl he had liked. She had been with him on the magazine committee in that last summer term. There had been five of them, he couldn't recall them very clearly, but he could remember her. They used to go outside and sit in the sun and read over articles and poems that had been submitted to them. He had an impression of a wall dappled with shadows. Funny how even that school had become more beautiful and nostalgic that summer, though in actual fact it was crude and dull. But that had been an enchanted summer.

And Richardson had been in charge of them. Not that he took much to do with them but now and again he would come and discuss a poem or two, mostly in order to criticise it fairly ruthlessly.

But Tom could remember it very clearly now. There had been a question of whether his own poems should be put in the magazine and he wanted them in, no question about that. He wanted to see his own name in print, though he knew that perhaps the magazine was not the most glorious aperture for viewing them by. But he had a desire which was almost hurtful in its intensity that the poems should be published. Though he thought that the others and especially Jean hadn't wanted them. Richardson too had looked at them briefly but had said nothing which was a sure sign that he didn't think much of them. He hadn't even bothered to criticise them. Tom could still see him reading them quickly and himself waiting for a verdict because it was so important to him. The poems were the most important things in the world to him at that time. He had only started writing, and he thought it was something he could do since he couldn't do very much else. All one needed was privacy and a pen and paper. But Richardson hadn't said anything at all. If Richardson had liked them then he would have known they were good and that would have been precious to him.

25

H E R E M E M B E R E D T H E day very well. It had been
a very hot summer's day and at dinner time he had come
into the school, into the coolness away from the dead glare.
He had wandered round the hall, jacketless, meeting no one.
The place seemed to lie in a dream of emptiness. He had
had a look at the defaced notices and had then climbed the
stairs to the balcony with a vague idea that he might find
the library open. But it wasn't, and he wandered aimlessly
along the balcony, now and again looking down into the hall
and for his own amusement turning his thumb down as if
he were gazing at phantom gladiators and he himself were
the Emperor. He came in his wanderings to the science room
and had gone in thinking that it would be cool there with all
the taps and glass and tubes. In fact he was bending over the
wash basin washing his face and hands which felt sticky
when he heard from a smallish room off the science room
sounds which were like strenuous sighings. Thinking for a
moment that they might be made by some of the juniors
who had gone in there and were engaged in horseplay, or
perhaps harming some equipment, he had gone over and
opened the door.

And there he saw them, that is, he saw Richardson lying
on top of her, that is, Jean, her legs clasped tightly round
his back, he with his face fastened to hers like a bird's
famished beak. Richardson was in his shirt (white), fastened,
probing, intent. Tom felt as if his face had been smashed in
like a window pane. He stood there astonished, confused,

in the grasp of a whirlwind of emotions, but above all what seemed to surge into his mind was not the immorality of the episode, it was the animality of it. It was the sight of the cool detached Richardson in that intense carnality, attached.

He stumbled away, pulling the door after him, not waiting to see what would happen, what Richardson would do, how he would extricate himself. He ran downwards lest Richardson should come after him, to explain, to talk. How could Richardson look at him now in class? It was lucky that he was leaving. How could he speak at all of the things of the mind now, how could he make his jokes? But Richardson would not pursue him, he knew. What after all could he say? "You know how it is, old chap"? No, Richardson didn't have the language of the squire to draw on.

His own head ached as if he wished to bury that sight, as if he wanted to walk again about the cool world, uncaring, free of responsibility. Without knowing what he was doing he got his jacket—which he had left in Richardson's room —and made his way steadily home as if he were walking against a high wind. At one stage he went into a café and bought himself an iced drink. When he got home he told his mother that he wasn't well—the heat, he said—and had fallen into a deep sleep still lying on the bed in his clothes.

He had in fact gone to school the following day, still suffering from the same headache, and the most amazing thing had happened. The two of them—he and Richardson —had decided as if by mutual empathy to ignore the whole thing. Richardson hadn't looked at him during the course of the lesson but had been rather more subdued than usual. He had looked slightly apprehensive, but knew perfectly well that Tom wouldn't say anything. It was a bit of a comedy really. But all the time Tom had a terrible headache and was shaking with terrible tremors like a land subject to earthquakes. He knew that something important and awful had happened, that he must survive it as best he might, that a precious thing like a vase had been irretrievably smashed, that time after time he would be visited by unutterable pain. Nor could he clearly focus why this should be. It was something to do with betrayal, with vulgarity, with hypocrisy expressed in its most animal form, with finding a rottenness at the centre of things in the most immediate manner, with seeing the world of his mother, frenzied and inferior, set here as well, a penetration of his final preserve.

So it was that night—after Richardson had told him just as he was going out of the room that his poems would be in the school magazine after all—that he lay down on his bed again, staring up at the ceiling, still suffering from the same intense blazing headache. His father was in the shed reading as usual, his mother was stamping heavily about the kitchen, he himself lay staring at the ceiling. He knew it would be impossible to carry on in the class as if nothing had happened even for the few remaining weeks, the situation was too intolerable and artificial, quite apart from the fact that he would have to see Jean every day and pretend that she had been totally invisible to him. He felt a bitter sense of betrayal. Behind the wit and the humour, behind the cool detachment, had been the same carnality and vulgarity which was at the centre of all things. There had been no superiority at all, only a false façade. All the other teachers—duller, more tedious—had been after all superior to Richardson. They had gone on their steady solid way doing their best, humourless, serious. He had misjudged them all. But more than all these speculations, not logically pursued, had been his vision of the animal body and the distortion of the detached mind.

And so the following morning he had taken his clothes and slipped quietly out of the house not knowing where he was going but determined to go somewhere. He had hitch-hiked his way north.

And now he was standing in the light of day in the cemetery looking around him. Dixon had been Richardson all the while and perhaps Ann had been Jean. How strange the ways of the mind were. And his so-called novel had been simply a method of psychological cure. Perhaps that was why he had such great difficulty with it. But why had Dixon become so objectionable, why had he come to hate him? Was that simply a psychological manifestation as well or did it mean something truer, more eternal? He knew now why he had run away from the hotel. It was because of that boy bending over Ann at the dance, suave, fair-haired, and a reminder of Dixon. He stood in the cemetery meditating. The stones sparkled in the chill light, names and dates standing out clearly in row after row. His mother was dead under one of those stones. Dixon for that matter was dead under all of them. Dixon was finished with forever. He would never write about him again, he would never feel anything for him but hate. All these ridiculous values, they had all been false.

He walked out of the cemetery quite briskly. He wanted to go home. He wanted to see Ann, to see what it was possible to salvage. Perhaps there was nothing to salvage, but at least he would try. Now he knew that he wasn't a writer, that that illusion was over, that he must save himself. He was willing to try to enter the world, it was necessary for him to do so, all the rest had been a dream.

26

It was afternoon when he approached his flat again and by a strange coincidence it was the time when Mrs Harrow in her patchy furs was setting out again on her usual trip. This time he did follow her, he didn't care whether he was seen or not. He wanted to find out once and for all whether her house existed. He waited till she had got on to the bus and got on behind her. She sat at the front and he at the back. He turned his face to the window and spent his time watching the people passing along the streets. He was thinking that it would be interesting if her dream turned out to be a reality. He wanted it to be reality. He wanted her to have succeeded with her project. For if she succeeded then he might succeed too in whatever he decided to do next. He couldn't continue with the life he was leading. That was quite settled in his mind. It would be pitiable, however, if she too turned out to be a figure of comedy, if she too had been living in a lie constructed out of her own psychological debris, especially when, as he looked out of the window, he could see so much of the city being rebuilt, the old slums being demolished, the tall new buildings taking their place.

When she eventually got out he followed her, past the university up a long street of largish houses. She turned in at one of them. Somehow she seemed to have become more brisk and effective and real as she approached the house, as if she was wearing a new authority. It was quite noticeable, something to do with her sense of purpose which communicated itself to her walk. If one has a purpose then one has everything, he thought. It doesn't matter what the purpose is, as long as one believes in it, then that of itself creates life. Even the rat has a purpose, the dog, the ant, the fly. Without purpose there is nothing at all, there is only fog, the sandy grit of tedium and emptiness that rubs at the eyes.

She entered and he followed her. He waited for a bit and then stood outside an open door. He heard her moving about in the room. Then he went into the room. She was standing looking up at a pair of purple curtains, admiring them. She swung round when he spoke. "Good afternoon, Mrs Harrow," he said. "I thought I'd come along and give you a hand. I saw you going in. I happened to be in the neighbourhood quite by chance. It really is amazing, isn't it?" She was astonished to see him as if he had broken into her private dream, but she gained control of herself rapidly.

"It's very beautiful," he said looking around him. And truly enough it was. The walls had been wallpapered in white, but the rest was purple throughout, curtains, chairs, carpets.

He said, "I'll give you a hand if you like."

"Do you think the students will like it?" she asked eagerly.

"I'm sure they will," he said. "I should like to stay here. It's very quiet." And it was too. He couldn't hear the sound of any traffic.

"This isn't all," she said suddenly. "There are other rooms. I have a bathroom and four bedrooms and a living room."

Her face had come alight, her clumsy body seemed to glow with achievement and pride of ownership. "I had to do something," she said, "when my husband ... It won't be long now till I get everything arranged. If you'd care to see

195

the other rooms. I was going to do some painting this afternoon. I have some paint pots in my bag here."

They walked into the other rooms, one of which still remained to do. The others were tastefully decorated each in a different colour, one in red, one in green. He felt as if he were in an art gallery walking from room to room admiring. How much she must have denied herself to do this!

"I thought," she said, "that I would call them the Purple Room, the Red Room and the Green Room. I got the idea from a magazine."

Tom suddenly felt that he wanted badly to do physical work again. He was tired of reading and writing. There was a part of him that felt starved after all those months. In the old days he had felt the same satisfaction when he had started work with a pick on a fine summer's morning and the stones of the road sparkled ahead of him, though the feeling had worn away in the course of the day with the pain and the tiredness. But at the beginning it was fine, that release of new areas of himself long unused.

"I should like to do some painting," he said. "I should like to help. I haven't got anything else to do anyway. Would you like me to do that?"

"It would be a great help," she said. "I'll go out and get some buns and rolls and I'll make tea later."

So she gave him the paint and the brushes and the turpentine and he spread on the floor some newspapers that she had brought. He had done some painting before though he wasn't a very good painter. Painting looked much easier than it really was. Still it was rather easier than wallpapering. All that stretch of wall waiting to be covered with yellow paint. For she had decided to call this the Yellow Room. He painted slowly and smoothly, feeling a kind of sleepy

rhythm permeate what he was doing. It was as if suddenly
he had decided that afternoon that he would let things
happen and not impose himself on them any more, as if he
had committed himself to the inevitable. He brushed with
a sleepy sensuous motion, aware only of the painting and
nothing else. He didn't wonder whether it was going to be
good or bad, he let it be what it was going to be. What he
did think of was that he was doing something useful, that he
was transforming a dull room without character into a pretty
room, that the room was being transformed under his eyes,
that moment by moment he was creating more and more
colour, that he liked what he was doing. He wanted to do
as much as possible, to tire himself out so that he would
sleep, he wanted to go on till he had finished, so that in fact
the lights were put on and he was still working in a dream
of satisfaction as more and more of the walls became yellow,
as less and less of them retained their drab dull white. He
ate his rolls and buns and drank his tea but he wouldn't
stop for long. He wanted to see the entire transformation
taking place, though now and again Mrs Harrow would say,
"Isn't it time for you to go home?" But even she began to
feel this as an adventure as, for the first time, she stayed on
late enough to put on the lights and see her house for the
first time in their glow. She fussed about with tea and
biscuits as he steadily worked on making the room sunnier
and sunnier. Some part of him was flowering in the paint,
some part of him had long needed this efflorescence into
reality, some part of him demanded this relentless, effortless
blossoming. He imagined at one stage that he was creating
a vast yellow flower, that he was himself this huge yellow
flower, that he was bringing into birth a new species. His
arm passed from aching to tranquillity. He no longer felt

tiredness when he stretched. He was like a remorseless god, intent and domestic. At one stage he found himself whistling a tune he thought he had forgotten, while Mrs Harrow watched him from the door, a smile on her lips.

When he was finally ready he said, "I think that's enough for now." And he stretched sensuously like a cat. He said, "Will you be all right now getting home?" She said yes, and he left her and went into a pub for a drink.

For the first time for many months he felt that he had deserved the drink. He drank his first pint slowly savouring it richly in his mouth. Then he bought another one. At one stage in the evening he got into a game of draughts with an old man who was smoking a pipe. The old man beat him easily.

"What you have to do," said the old man, "is gain control of the centre. That's what you have to do. You're always out on the flanks. Gain control of the centre." The old man puffed smoke contentedly.

"I think I'll get married," said Tom for no reason at all, after he had lost the game.

The old man looked at him through clouds of smoke. "Merrit, eh? Are ye no merrit yet?"

"No," said Tom. "But I think I shall get married." He felt warm and happy and slightly drunk.

The old man was quiet for a while, then he said, "It's a big step in a man's life. I've been merrit thirty-six year." He added, "I'm here every night of the week."

"What?" said Tom. "You mean you leave the house every night and come and sit here? What does your wife do?"

"My wife has to put up with it," he said. "Son, when I was your age, if my wife looked at any other man I'd clobber

198

him. We used to fight each other all the time, all the time. I clobbered a bloke once for smiling at her, a stranger he was. Mind you, I didna like him. We was in this bar and he was sitting at the other end of the bar by hisself, and he smiled at my wife and I went over and clobbered him. But that's all gone now. Now I know she'll be waiting for me and I'll be waiting for her."

"In here?" said Tom.

"She knows where A am," said the old man comfortably. "She knows where A am. She's the best wife any man could have."

The bar began to fill up and there was no room any longer to play draughts. Tom found himself sitting at a table with the old man and a lot of other people who seemed to be in a group. Two of them started a long discussion on Marx and the UCS.

One of them was saying, "What Marx means by the dictatorship of the proletariat is that the working classes— that's me and you—will take over in the end."

"I agree wi' ye," said the other man who had a small black thin moustache and looked like a film star whose name Tom couldn't remember. "I agree wi' ye, but you haveta remember that the Chinks did it wi'oot a proper proletariat."

"You could do it yourself wi'oot a proper proletariat," said the first man who burst out laughing. He turned round to the others and said, "Imagine old Ken here doing it wi' a' the proletariat standing roon. Aw, bugger off."

The old man had told them that Tom was thinking of getting married, and he found himself surrounded by people offering him drinks, advice and jokes.

At a little after ten o'clock he was standing outside the pub saying goodbye to a lot of new hazy friends, swaying on his feet, and laughing a great deal.

He floated off eventually, waving his arms and saying, "Goo' night, sweet ladies, goo' night. Goo' night sweet Lil," he shouted after a large man with a broken nose who worked in a shipyard. "Goo' night Desperate Dan," he shouted, swaying, "goo' night my red comics."

Staggering from side to side he set off home.

27

A S H E W A L K E D along he suddenly found an unshaven bristly dirty man, who seemed to be wearing long dirty skirts belted by a rope, slanting along beside him. This vague tall being kept pace with him all the time, greyish, foggy, like the survivor of a war.

"Who are you?" said Tom. "What do you want?"

He thought of him as one of the innumerable outcasts of the city scrabbling among ruined buildings and pleading for VP or spirits.

But the man said nothing, still keeping pace with him all the time, while a strong rank smell compounded of wet cloth and sickness and cheap spirits emanated from him, so that Tom began to feel panicky. Would the man attack him? Would he hit him over the head and try to take what little money he had from him and then retreat to whatever cave or slum he inhabited? The night was now quite dark and he could hardly see him, only he had an impression of greyness and bristle and long flapping clothes. Now and again the man would try to put his hand on his shoulder as if pleading with him for something. Perhaps—greatest of horrors—he had recognised a being like himself. Perhaps he was dumb and was trying to communicate without speech. Tom began to run and the man ran with him alongside him, panting, or at least he lengthened his stride in such a manner that Tom couldn't draw away from him. He felt dirty and stained as if he were being infected by this being which moved alongside him as if it were a huge bird of prey whose breath smelt of corruption and carrion.

Tom was sober again, his gaiety had left him, his sense of irresponsible joy was dissipated and he felt again in touch with a kind of reality, a grey shrouded smelly bristly reality. Were the man's hands really hands or were they claws? What should he do? Should he try to speak to it?

Words began to spout out of him almost against his will. "Who are you? What do you want? How do you spend your time?" All these questions he asked as if he were begging pardon, as if he were acknowledging responsibility.

Tom used to see people like this shambling along the roads with bags over their shoulders or sitting half asleep in reading rooms. Who were these people? Where had they come from? Once in broad daylight he had seen a chimney sweep on a bicycle cycling decorously along wearing black shiny clothes, the face black, a comic Death.

He felt despair emanating from the figure like slime. Oh God, he thought, if only it were daylight. If only the dawn would come up, if only he were in the Yellow Room again painting.

He felt the panting of the figure again as if it were out of condition. What did it want of him? It did not seem to wish to attack him, otherwise it would have done so before. It merely wanted to be with him, walking beside him. Sometimes under street lights he could see the thin bluish face, the whiskers, the thin bony hands.

After a while a kind of peace came over him. Perhaps the being just wanted companionship, perhaps that was all it wanted. Perhaps it just wanted the smell and the touch of man. Perhaps it just wanted to be near the sound of his footsteps. Was that so monstrous a crime?

The city was full of people like this, escaped from the

bright bubble of the Welfare State, from its air suit. It slanted along beside him, as the dog trotted beside the other old man, but silent, not barking, not making a sound except that now and again it panted as if Tom were walking too fast.

Eventually it stopped as if it could go on no longer. Tom looked at it for a moment, that being assembled from layer after layer of old flesh and old cloth and outdated newspapers, wondering what he should do. But he knew that there was nothing really that he could do. He put his hands despairingly in his pockets and pulled out the last silver he had and pushed it into the claws. Then he hurried on. The being, composed of greyish fog, lifted its hand in a feeble wave, and as it did so the money poured out of the hand and dropped on to the road.

Tom walked on, looking around him from time to time in case duplicates of the being would emerge out of the night, but none came. The night was in fact astonishingly quiet. He saw again as if ahead of him the two Jehovah's Witnesses clad in their streaming plastic, as if fresh from space, and saying, "What do you think about life?"

When he reached his flat it seemed as if he had been away for centuries. He stared at the room where he worked as if he did not recognise it. There were books lying on the floor. There was a mass of typescript. The harsh light of the bulb beat down on the carpet.

He got hold of the typescript and systematically began to tear it into little pieces which he scattered like confetti into the bucket ready to be put out in the morning. He looked at the clock but it had stopped. He thought it must be about eleven o'clock at night, but he did not know for sure. He suddenly felt very tired and prepared for bed.

He gazed at the yellow bottle of Parozone. If only one

could wash the whole world clean with that acid, he thought, if only one could pour it over all the stains so that everything would become clear and clean again. But the yellow bottle of Parozone remained where it was, inscrutable, immune, bearing nothing on its surface, not even a picture, brutally self-sufficient.

He went to bed and fell asleep almost immediately though the sheets were cold.

28

A N N K N E W T H A T Tom would come and see her. The night he had abruptly left her she had cried a lot but had insisted that she get a taxi; she refused the offer of a lift from the boy she was dancing with. She hadn't spoken to Mary about what had happened, but had been wholly miserable. She hadn't gone to Tom's flat out of pride though once or twice she had dressed herself to go. Yet all the time in spite of her wretchedness she had known that he would come. She knew more about him than she knew about herself.

When she thought of him she didn't at all see a future writer of distinction. She saw only a boy who nearly always looked untidy, needed someone to look after him, was unhappy. She didn't think at all about his writing, she wondered mostly whether he was eating enough, and whether he kept his flat tidy. She didn't require anything exceptional from him—she didn't think in those terms—though she feared sometimes that he might require something exceptional from her. At first when he had met her she hadn't been taken with him. She hadn't missed him when he had left her at first, or when he wasn't with her. Later, however, this had changed and she had missed him. It was as if she was no longer wholly herself, wholly present in the immediate world, but rather as if she were two people in her skin, for both of whom she was responsible. If it was love that she felt then love was different from what she had expected it would be. As a schoolgirl she had thought that love was a vast radiance that surrounded the lovers, in which they moved as fish move through the seas, their natural element. Now she was beginning to think that love was not like that at all. Love was an ache that was constituted by an absence.

Quite realistically she knew that if she didn't marry Tom she wouldn't marry at all. She knew that no one else would demand so much of her. She had no one else and he had no one else. He could, she thought, even now apply for a training college or a university. She knew that he would be happier that way.

When he had left her stumbling into the night she had been very hurt and had cried. It was the first time that she had cried for such a reason, it was wholly involuntary and inexplicable. She felt that he had been unfair since he had asked her to stay for the dance and she had waited because he had wanted her to wait. The tears perhaps were tears of offended pride and dignity, but she felt that perhaps they were more than that. They were an acceptance of a union not yet achieved.

She knew that she might suffer from these jealousies later but she also knew that it was better to be with him than to be without him. That, she realised, was what love meant. It was funny that it hadn't touched her before, that this emotion so apparently common had avoided her. She had read somewhere of office girls who, after a broken love affair, would weep uncontrollably and be unfit to work, but she had never thought that was anything but a strange romantic delusion.

She began to imagine a possible future but couldn't really do so. The future would be what it became. She could continue to teach and he would find a job. They would have to buy a house. She thought of practical things like that and as she thought of them they became more specific. They might even have children. They would have friends perhaps on whom they might call and who might call on them. That was what living was about. They would learn to plan things together. They would be together because it was necessary for them to be together.

She felt that he would come soon, that even that morning he was on his way towards her, that he wouldn't be able to stay away. She thought that he might come to the school and waited for him the whole morning though she carried on with her work, since one must always do that no matter what one's private griefs are. But he didn't come either in the morning or in the afternoon. She sat and watched TV when she came home, Mary being out with one of her innumerable boy friends. Now she couldn't imagine how such promiscuity was possible. She couldn't conceive of such a multiplicity, as if people were things. She couldn't keep her attention on the TV programme and would restlessly get up from the chair and go to the window hoping that she would see him.

She made herself innumerable cups of tea. She tried to do some work but found she couldn't concentrate. Once or twice she went to the mirror to see how she looked and saw that there were wrinkles above her brow. She thought : If he doesn't come, this is what my life will be like. And she felt such despair that she nearly cried. But she gritted her teeth and didn't allow herself to. What was important was to have another human being with whom one could share one's thoughts, one's griefs, one's joys.

It was six o'clock when the doorbell rang. She got up, waited for what seemed an eternity to test her will, and walked slowly to the door, giving an almost final look at the room, as if she wouldn't see it again, or not again in the same way. It was almost as if she had changed totally in the moments between hearing the bell and reaching the door.

He was there waiting. She opened the door and he came in. When he was in she shut the door and they put their arms around each other without speaking. They stood like that for a long time, as if they would weep but didn't.

Later on they watched TV and the story seemed to be more interesting than she thought. Continually she saw in it reminders of her own life, past and present. She felt Tom looking at her as she moved about the room and made tea. She was conscious of being the person he would be looking at for a long time, for many years, and because of this she blossomed anew. Something about him told her that a crisis was past, that he had in some sense found himself, that he was ready to leave for another world, another place. That he was ready to be with her. There was about him the gaunt air of beginnings.